"Will our marriage be strictly business?"

Amber uttered the question, then forced herself to meet Joel's glance squarely, reminding herself how desperately she needed his money.

"By which, I take it, you mean no sex?" he countered coolly.

"But, of course, Amber. I thought I'd made that plain; even if you were Venus herself, you'd be perfectly safe. Mercenary women have no appeal for me—in fact they turn me off. And your charms—" his eyes flicked cruelly over her too-thin body before turning to her paper-white face "—such as they are, are not sufficient to change my mind. In public we will be newly married lovers but I, for one, will not forget that it's just a charade."

D0696748

PENNY JORDAN
is also the author of these

Harlequin Presents

Many of these books are available at your local bookseller.

For a free catalog listing all titles currently available,
send your name and address to:

HARLEQUIN READER SERVICE
1440 South Priest Drive, Tempe, AZ 85281
Canadian address: Stratford, Ontario N5A 6W2

PENNY JORDAN

the flawed marriage

Harlequin Books

TORONTO • NEW YORK • LOS ANGELES • LONDON
AMSTERDAM • PARIS • SYDNEY • HAMBURG
STOCKHOLM • ATHENS • TOKYO • MILAN

Harlequin Presents first edition April 1983
ISBN 0-373-10584-3

Original hardcover edition published in 1983
by Mills & Boon Limited

Printed in U.S.A.

CHAPTER ONE

IT was cold and damp. The mist, which had been no more than tiny wisps veiling the highest peaks of the Lakeland mountains on her journey to the children's home earlier that afternoon, had now descended as far as the road she was walking along, Amber noticed wearily. It was also growing dark; a strange eerie darkness, unlike the city twilight she was more accustomed to. She shivered, drawing her thin suede coat closer around her almost too angular body, her right leg dragging slightly as she tried to increase her walking pace. Her leg. She grimaced to herself as she glanced impotently at the limb she was fast coming to consider the author of all her misfortunes, including this latest unsuccessful attempt to obtain a job. She had been so full of hope when she set out from Birmingham this morning, buoying herself up during the long train ride by reminding herself of the excellence of her qualifications. Not only was she a fully qualified teacher, but she also had over a year's nursing experience. Her eyes went involuntarily to her leg again. Six months now since the accident; six months! It seemed to Amber that six centuries separated the happy, fulfilled girl of twenty she had been from the bitter, maimed person she was now, and the irony of the whole thing was that it needn't have happened at all.

She had been on her way to work at the time.

Having qualified as a teacher, she had left university just in time to find herself a victim of local government education cuts, and so instead had decided to train as a nurse. Rob had been full of approval. He was on the point of finishing his own medical training—he wanted to go into private practice, though, which meant specialising, a costly business both in terms of money and time, but with Amber working as a nurse they should be able to bring the date of their wedding forward. That was what Amber had been thinking about as she walked to the large hospital on her way to work. She didn't have to walk very far, living as she did in a nearby student nurses' home, and her mind had been on Rob and his bombshell of the previous evening—that he intended to go out to Saudi Arabia to work for two years. He had been offered a plum job as assistant to an eminent plastic surgeon working in the Middle East, a chance he simply could not afford to pass up, as he had earnestly explained to Amber. She had been dismayed by his news. They had met at university and she had known that because of Rob's chosen career it would be several years before they could marry, but she had visualised him specialising at one of the large Birmingham hospitals—not thousands of miles away.

She had noticed the bus stopping ahead of her as an automatic reflex action; the giggling children disgorged on to the pavement; the small yellow-raincoated little girl stepping out behind the bus; the car speeding towards her. Her reaction had been automatic, and ridiculously unnecessary. The child—streetwise—had managed to avoid the skidding wheels of the car, and it was Amber, who had so recklessly gone to her rescue, who had been tossed like a rag doll to lie inert and unconscious in the road.

She had been lucky, or so they tried to convince her, but Amber didn't consider a leg which because of its torn and destroyed muscles might never move properly again to be something to feel grateful for, and had said so, even when the surgeon told her gravely that she was lucky to have it, and that there had been talk of amputation. And there were also the scars; horrible, maiming scars, running along the slender length of her thigh and marring the slender perfection of her calf. At first she had refused to accept the truth; she would walk properly again. But it was six months now since the accident and she knew that no amount of willpower was ever going to restore her right leg to the lithe manoeuvrability it had once had. There was a slight chance, Mr Savage, the consultant, had told her when she demanded to be told the truth; a very risky and highly technical operation only available in America, but it cost many thousands of pounds, and was not guaranteed to be successful, and then there would be the plastic surgery to remove her scars.

Rob had been understanding at first, but then there had been those evenings when he had not visited her; those conversations about the necessity of a successful society doctor having a glamorous, elegant wife. He hadn't needed to labour the point. Amber had understood, and when she offered to call things off, he had agreed without protest. That night after he had gone had been the first time she had cried. She had never felt more alone in her life. Who did she have to turn to? Her father had died when she was eight and her mother had remarried while Amber was at university. She liked her stepfather, but they weren't a close family. Her mother was easily upset and had wept bitterly on the one occasion she had come to visit Amber in hospital. It had been impossible for her to go on working at the hospital; hence the necessity for her journey here today to the Lake District. The moment she had seen the advertisement for a junior housemother at a children's home, her hopes had started to rise. They had been most enthusiastic over the telephone; right up until the moment they had seen her, in fact.

Like sharp knives she could clearly recall the interviewer's voice, pitying but firm, as she explained that whoever got the job would need to be agile and tireless—looking after about twenty-five children ranging from thirteen downwards was a very demanding job. And not suitable for a cripple, Amber told herself bitterly.

She shivered suddenly as the mist reached out damp tendrils towards her. Who would guess that it was May? It was cold enough to be the middle of winter. Of course, it was pretty high up here, and if she hadn't lingered to watch the trout in the mountain stream she wouldn't have missed her bus, and there would have been no necessity for her to trudge down this seemingly endless road, although she distinctly remembered seeing a sign in the village on the way up announcing that it was merely a mile and a half to Inchmere House, the children's home.

Gritting her teeth against the nagging pain from her torn muscles, she kept on walking. Pain was something she had grown used to living with. The doctors had prescribed various drugs, but she had refused them. Sometimes she thought the only thing that kept her going was her constant battle not to give in. She had been so full of hope this morning. The job would have provided her with a means of earning her living and a roof over her head, both important considerations, as since leaving the hospital she had been depleting her small savings on the rent of a shabby, chilly room in a Birmingham boarding house, and the necessities of day-to-day living.

She could have turned to her mother, but pride had prevented her; the same pride which had forced her to smile and look pleased when her mother announced her stepfather's plans for retirement in Spain. In another two weeks they would be gone, and then she would be completely on her own.

Weak tears of self-pity welled in her eyes and she dashed them away angrily. It was pointless thinking about what was past; she could never have lived with her parents anyway, even if they had offered her a home. But she had to get a job; some means of earning money—any means of earning money!

Like an Eldorado the surgeon's words lured her on; the memory of his advice that there was an operation which could restore her leg to full strength, the frail hope she had clung to in the weeks after Rob's defection; weeks when she battled daily with a swamping sense of rejection and bitterness, telling herself that once restored to her old self she would show Rob what he had lost by deserting her when she needed him most! Her hands curled into her palms, bitterness etched in the magnificent tawny eyes which had given rise to her unusual name. Tiger eyes, Rob had lovingly called them, going on to whisper passionately that he loved them just as he loved everything about her. But no one would whisper words of love to her now! She shuddered suddenly with cold, the sleek length of her dark gold hair plastered to her neck by the damp air, her too thin body telling its own story of illness and neglect.

Rob. She closed her eyes momentarily, overwhelmed by weakness. How she longed for him at this moment—the warmth of his arms; the sweet tenderness of his kisses—a tenderness which had promised to ripen into passion, but time and circumstances had always been against them. Amber refused to have her first experience of total possession spoiled by being rushed or being conducted unromantically. Rob had laughed at her, but he hadn't argued. They had been planning to go away together for a week's holiday before the Saudi business came up, and she had bought, in anticipation of the holiday, brief wisps of underwear, and a soft, feminine nightdress that had been far too expensive, but irresistible.

Lost in the past, she didn't hear the warning sound heralding the approach of a car, and her first intimation of its intrusion was the loud blaring of its horn.

Time rolled back and she was held fast, transfixed in the beam of powerful fog lights, frozen and unable to move, her face a pale, fearful oval caught in the powerful lights for a brief second before the car swerved across the road and up the banking, and the engine was suddenly cut.

The sudden cessation of sound broke through her wall of terror, and moving awkwardly, Amber stumbled to the side of the road. Behind her she heard a car door open, and brisk hard footsteps. Impelled by a fierce urgency to escape, she pressed on, almost running, her cry of pain as hard fingers grasped her shoulder swallowed up by the curling mist.

'What the hell's the matter with you? Why didn't you move? Got a death wish, have you?'

The harsh male voice filled her senses, rasping against over-sensitised nerves. Her assailant was practically shaking her, her damp hair falling against her face, concealing it from him. With a sudden impatient movement he grasped it, pushing it away and forcing her face up.

'Well, well!' he breathed sardonically when he saw her too finely drawn features and the cheekbones made prominent by lack of nourishing food. 'What a waif and stray it is! What were you trying to do? Seek oblivion under my car wheels?'

'And if I was?' Amber flared at him, suddenly too angry to bother denying his mocking comment.

'Then you're a fool,' came the crisp retort. 'Life is for living, little miss waif and stray, not for throwing away. That's something you learn early up here amongst the mountains. Not local, are you?' he asked, giving her unsuitable coat and city shoes a dry and cursory glance. 'What are you doing up here? Hired one of the holiday cottages and had a tiff with the boy-friend?'

Amber's chin tilted defiantly, and she longed for the mist to lift and the dark landscape to be illuminated so that she could let this insufferable stranger see the contempt in her eyes.

'Nothing so juvenile. No *man* is worth killing oneself for.'

'So what are you doing up here? Taking a quiet stroll?'

The sarcastic retort stung.

'If you must know, I was looking for a job—at the children's home.'

'And because you didn't get it you decided to fling yourself under my wheels. Bit drastic, wasn't it?'

It was sheer exasperation that made her retort crossly, 'Oh, don't be so ridiculous! I wasn't throwing myself under your wheels at all. If you must know I . . .' She stopped abruptly, remembering how she had just stood frozen in the beam of his lights, and changed her tack, to say accusingly, 'You shouldn't have been driving so fast. You could have caused an accident. Drivers never think of pedestrians.' A trace of bitterness crept unknowingly into her voice. 'They don't care what risks they take with other people's lives, and when they do, they get away scot free . . .'

'What are you implying? That I owe you compensation? You've been watching too much American television, lady, and you've got it wrong. The car has to actually touch you before you can claim.'

'And even then you don't always get anything,' Amber said coolly, remembering her own inability to claim compensation from the driver who had injured her, despite the fact that he had been speeding, because he had not been properly insured.

She remembered that she was not wearing a watch, and that the last train for her connection left the village at eight-thirty. She had no idea what time it was now. She had left the home at seven and seemed to have been walking for hours.

'Could you tell me the time, please?' she asked quickly. 'I have a train to catch.'

She saw the glint of gold on a lean male wrist clad in a dark jacket which seemed to be of a leather fabric, although because of his dark clothes, Amber could make out very little of her companion's appearance apart from the fact that he was tall, with dark hair.

'Just gone eight,' he told her laconically.

Eight! She tried to fight down a sense of panic. She only had a few pounds in her purse. If she missed her connection she would have to wait until morning, which meant finding somewhere to stay.

'Thank you. I must go . . .' Without waiting to see his reaction she started to hurry down the road, for once not concerned with what the man watching her might think of her ungainly gait.

She heard the car door slam seconds after she had left him, and knew from the brevity of time which had elapsed that he had not spent much time watching her, and an irrational feeling of resentment filled her. He might at least have offered to run her into the village, even if it was in the opposite direction to that he was taking.

But why should he? Perhaps if she had been the girl she used to be he might have found her attractive enough to have offered her a lift—but then the girl she had been would not have needed one.

She was so intent on hurrying, so deep in her thoughts, that she didn't hear the soft purr of the car engine untl it drew level with her, and the now familiar hard voice drawled, 'Get in. I'll take you to the station.'

The passenger door was thrust open, the interior light coming on to reveal the opulent luxury of cream hide seats and a thick matching carpet. The light which illuminated the car interior also revealed the features of its owner, and Amber caught her breath in mingled awe and uncertainty.

Handsome wasn't the word it was possible to use in connection with this man, she admitted as she limped awkwardly towards the open door. Striking, sensually compelling; intensely male; these were the words with which to describe the hooded grey eyes which swept her with predatory intentness, assessing and dismissing her feminine appeal, the aquiline profile turned autocratically towards her.

'You're limping.' The words held none of the pity she had grown accustomed to and withdrawn from in the long dark days since her accident, and just as she registered that fact he leaned across the passenger seat, long fingers grasping her wrist as she was pulled effortlessly into the warm interior of the car, and the door firmly closed behind her, rather as though she were an irritating child unable to fend for herself.

'How did it happen?'

He was watching her intently, the cool grey gaze sending frissons of awareness flickering her body. The old Amber would have described him as a very male and attractive man, but the new embittered Amber saw only the hard purpose in the depths of the grey eyes fixed upon her white face, and knew a shuddering desire to escape from the too intimate environs of the car and the disturbing proximity of its owner. Only the knowledge that without his offer of a lift she could well miss her train prevented her from quitting the car immediately. As always when her limp was mentioned she stiffened involuntarily, her face closing up, the huge golden eyes shadowed and shuttered.

'An accident,' she told him tonelessly. 'Do you live locally?'

'Relatively speaking. What sort of accident?' he asked smoothly, refusing to allow her to change the subject.

'I was hit by a car—driven too fast.'

'Which makes your carelessness of a few moments ago all the more foolhardy.'

'Only if you happen to be a speed-crazed maniac,' Amber snapped back.

The dark eyebrows rose, reinforcing the almost demonic features of the man opposite her, his mouth curling downwards sardonically as he scrutinised her.

'Speed-crazed? Oh, I hardly think so,' he offered. 'Forty isn't considered excessive on these roads—not when one knows them.'

Which meant that he must live locally, Amber reflected, even though he hadn't answered her earlier question.

'Even in thick fog?' she demanded, refusing to cede victory.

'A little mist,' her companion scoffed, deftly navigating a series of tortuous hairpin bends. 'You said you were up here for an interview for a job. Why? You aren't a local.'

'I wasn't aware that was another prerequisite,'

Amber began sarcastically, a little dismayed by the alert, 'Another? Why, what was the other?' that he fired at her.

Exhaustion and depression forced down her guard, allowing a little of the bitterness she normally kept bottled up inside her to spill over her iron control.

'Can't you guess? I should have thought a man of your perception would have realised immediately. As you so sapiently mentioned earlier, I limp.'

'And because of that you were turned down for the job?'

Although all his concentration was on the road and the powerful car, Amber felt his sideways glance, probing the thin skin barely covering her emotional scars.

'Although my qualifications were good, as a junior housemistress they wanted something more mobile.'

'Junior housemistress? That would have been a living-in position, surely, and a time-consuming one.' She felt him looking at her ringless fingers and guessed the mental assessment he was making. Single, and likely to remain so through circumstances rather than choice: an object of pity and derision.

'So what will you do now?'

Cold and shaken by her experience both at the interview and afterwards, Amber made an attempt to shrug unconcernedly and failed pitifully.

'I don't know. I just wish I did,' she muttered under her breath, not intending the words to be overheard, but his hearing was obviously as acute as a predatory hunter's, because his head swivelled towards her, and the car slid to a smooth halt in a small layby, across the bridge from the village. Thinking that he had taken her as far as he meant to, Amber reached for the door handle, but he stopped her, reaching across her body to grasp her hand. Amber shrank from him instinctively. She had learned in hospital that although she might be an object of medical interest and curiosity to the young doctors clustering daily around her bed, as a desirable and attractive woman she no longer existed; pity rather than admiration was what she read in their eyes; a pity that she had seen time and time again in the months that had followed. From taking the vibrant beauty which had been a facet of her personality before the accident for granted, she had retreated into a world where her beauty had been dimmed by pain and loss of self-confidence. If Rob could no longer find her attractive how could any man? Unwittingly over the weeks she had adopted the mien and shrinking manners of a girl who knows herself unattractive to men, and so she shrank now; not from any fear that her companion might touch her but from his assumption that she might want him to do so and the humiliation of rejection which must surely follow.

'What's the matter?'

There was a fine thread of amusement woven into the conventional words, a smile deepening the attractive grooves either side of a mouth which looked as though it didn't smile often enough. 'Having second thoughts about the wisdom of accepting a lift? Too late, fair maiden,' he mocked. 'I have you within my toils now, and there's no one to stop me having my wicked way with you. Tell me about your life before this accident,' he demanded with an abrupt change of front.

'What on earth for? Look, I must go, otherwise I'll miss my train.' Amber reached again for the door handle, only to find the door immovable beneath her urgent fingers.

'I've locked it.' He motioned towards the highly technical-looking dashboard. 'And I won't unlock it until you've answered my questions.'

'But why? What possible interest could you have in me?'

'The very natural one of a prospective employer,' came the totally unexpected reply. 'I need someone to look after my son.'

'How old is he?' Ridiculously it was the first question which came into her mind.

'Six.'

'But why should you want to employ me? Before this evening we hadn't even met. I don't even know your name . . .'

'That's easily remedied. I'm Joel Sinclair. I live about eight miles away from here.'

'And you need someone to look after your son. Surely a fully trained nanny would be better? And your wife . . .'

He was shaking his head.

'I've made up my mind that you'll be ideal. What's your name?'

Hesitantly, hardly daring to believe that the day might after all have have some benefit for her, Amber told him.

'Amber? Because of your eyes, of course.'

She blinked at him, surprised that he had noticed. Rob had been going out with her for over a month before he had made the connection.

'Mr Sinclair, are you sure? About this job, I mean?' she asked formally. 'You aren't just ...' she fumbled for the right words, hating the thought that he might have offered her the job on impulse because of some misguided feeling of pity.

'Sorry for you?' His face hardened. 'When you get to know me better you'll learn that there isn't room in my life for such unnecessary emotions.'

'Well, hadn't I better meet your son before we settle anything? I mean, he might not ...' She was glancing down at her leg, and she saw that he too was looking at the frail limb.

'Oh, he'll like you all right,' came the response. 'So, do I take it you're prepared to accept the job?'

A tiny frown touched Amber's forehead. He seemed to be treating the whole affair far too lightly. After all, what did he know about her, apart from what she had told him? What did she know about him, come to that? She moistened her lips, darting a quick glance up at him, dismayed to find him watching her with sardonic amusement.

'It all seems so ... so unconventional. I mean, you've just met me and you offer me the job of taking care of your son without asking for references, without ...'

'I know all I want to know,' he told her, cutting her short, 'In fact, Amber Douglas, you're something in the nature of a gift from the gods.' His laughter shocked and hurt her, although she tried to conceal it. Rob had thought her a gift from the gods once, but not in the same terms as Joel Sinclair, who only saw in her twisted leg a flaw which would probably make her pathetically grateful for his offer of a job.

'But we haven't discussed terms,' she said uneasily. 'A contract . . .'

'Don't worry,' he told her suavely, 'you'll have a contract; and you'll be well paid. Now, are you interested, or shall I drive across the bridge so that you can escape on the train that's due in any moment now?'

Well paid! Amber knew that he hadn't missed her expression of indecision. Goodness knows, she needed all the money she could get her hands on, and presumably she'd be living all found. She wanted to ask him exactly what he would be prepared to pay her, but pride—and the look in his eyes—prevented her.

She took a deep breath.

'I'm interested.'

'Good.' He switched on the engine. 'In that case, I'll take you up to Lake Fyne now, so that you can meet Paul first-hand.'

She thought about the long journey back to Birmingham, the cold, inhospitable room waiting for her, and then darted a glance at the man sitting beside her.

'Any objections?'

Without giving herself time to think she shook her head, feeling the powerful surge of the engine as the car pulled swiftly away, and the darkness swallowed them up.

Joel Sinclair had told her that he lived eight miles from the village, but it might as well have been eighty for all the sense of direction Amber experienced on the drive. Mist swirled all around them; the odd sheep materialising in the powerful headlights as they swept the grey blankness of the road, and the now frost-rimed hillsides stretching uproads from the tarmac.

Lake Fyne! She couldn't remember ever hearing the name before, but then she knew that the Lake District possessed many small lakes whose names were not universally known, and she assumed this must be one of them.

The road curled upwards, a pale grey ribbon, disappearing into the mist.

Sitting on the edge of her seat, gripping the expensive hide cover, Amber was unaware of the fear in her eyes, until Joel turned towards her mockingly, commanding her to relax, telling her there was nothing to fear.

What did he know? she demanded inwardly in a flash of irritation. He had never had to face people with her disability to see the expression in their eyes. She had yet to be accepted by his son and his wife. She could just picture her; a man like him would demand sophistication and elegance in the woman who bore his name; she would be blonde, almost undoubtedly; expensively dressed, an ex-model perhaps, who would raise her eyebrows pityingly when she saw the stray waif her husband had brought home.

They came to an abrupt halt. The mist lifted momentarily and Amber had a brief glimpse of moonlight on water—Lake Fyne?—and then they were driving through huge wrought iron gates which had opened as though at some magic command from Joel to allow the car to move smoothly down a gravel drive towards, the grey granite house slowly materialising ahead of them out of the mist.

Joel, stopped the car. The silence was almost uncanny, heavy, and somehow waiting. There were no lights from the house, and Amber presumed that there must be rooms overlooking the back, where no doubt his wife eagerly awaited his return.

He climbed out of the car, and for one awful moment Amber thought he intended to leave her, but even as she moved frantically towards her door, he was opening it, assisting her to alight, his fingers hard and warm beneath her elbow.

Gravel crunched underfoot. The house was huge, Victorian and austere, and Amber shivered as she waited for Joel to unlock the door.

'Housekeeper's night off,' he told her with heavy irony as the door swung open and he ushered her into a large but cold hall. He saw her shiver and told her, 'Mrs Downs is Lakeland born and bred and thinks central heating should be kept only for the depths of winter.' He glanced at his watch. 'It's too late for you to see Paul tonight, he'll be asleep, so I'll show you to a room, and then in the morning . . .'

'But surely your wife will want . . .' Amber began, only to be silenced by the look of grim mockery she saw on his face.

'Ah yes, my wife. Well, you see, my dear Amber, I no longer have a wife, which is why I need you— to take her place.'

The room reeled. Amber placed her hands to her head, telling herself that she was leaping to absurd conclusions.

'You mean you need someone to look after Paul full time because you don't have a wife?' she said hesitantly, her heart starting to sink when saw him dislodge himself from the wall upon which he had been leaning and come towards her, his hands on her shoulders as he pulled her forward into the harsh overhead light of the hall.

'What I mean, Amber,' he said slowly and coolly, 'is that I need a wife. Not just any wife, but you.'

'You must be mad!'

He seemed amused rather than affronted.

'Not mad, just determined. Determined that my ex-wife won't revoke the custody ruling which gave Paul into my care. So determined, in fact, that I am prepared to pay you very generously for say, six months of your life ... Very generously,' he repeated significantly, his eyes resting on the tell-tale pulse throbbing in her throat.

'No!'

'No?' Again he seemed more amused than annoyed. 'I'm going to give you the night to think over your decision, Amber, and don't forget, will you, that I saw the look on your face in the car when I said I was prepared to be generous.'

Hating herself for the question, but knowing she just had to ask it, Amber ran her tongue nervously across dry lips and asked huskily, 'How generous?'

She almost missed the surprised contempt in his eyes—it was banished so quickly by mocking satisfaction.

'Twenty-five thousand pounds!'

Her heart almost stopped beating. Twenty-five thousand pounds—far, far more than she had imagined. Far, far more than she could ever envisage earning in so short a space of time, and more than enough to cover all the expenses of her operation, plus the plastic surgery she would need afterwards.

'You can't do it,' a tiny inner voice warned her. 'It isn't right. You'll have to refuse.'

The words were on the tip of her tongue when she looked down at her leg and all her good resolutions fled. What were six months, after all?

'It would have to be purely a business arrangement,' she began hesitantly. 'I mean . . .'

'I think we can take what you mean as read,' came the smooth rejoinder, 'and certainly I can assure you that I have no sexual designs upon your person, if that's what's worrying you.'

Amber flushed to the roots of her hair. Of course he hadn't. What man in his right mind would have, never mind a man as stunningly attractive as Joel Sinclair?

Chagrined, exhausted and defeated by her own desire to be restored to what she had once been, she gave in.

'Very wise,' Joel Sinclair told her softly. 'I *am* glad we were able to reach an agreement. Tell me, the money—do you need it for any special purpose?'

In a moment he might guess about her leg, and Amber couldn't bear his pity. Quickly she interrupted, 'No more special than any other woman's. I want to enjoy life before it's too late. I've always fancied a world cruise . . .'

'With the bonus of some gullible male thrown in?' Joel Sinclair suggested sardonically. 'Still, why should I complain? In this instance your mercenary greed is furthering my ends as well as yours. I'll take you to your room now,' he told her. 'I have to go out again—some business I have to attend to, but in the morning we'll talk again.'

They had reached a long landing and he had paused outside a panelled mahogany door, and

Amber had almost collided into him before she realised he had stopped.

He opened the door and stood back to allow her to enter the room. It was furnished with timelessly elegant Regency antiques, but despite the expensive furniture, the soft pale green carpet and daintily femine décor the room had a cold almost unwelcoming atmosphere, and Amber shivered as she stepped inside it.

'The bathroom's through there,' Joel Sinclair told her, indicating another door opening off the bedroom. 'We normally have breakfast about eight. I have business interests in Kendal and try to leave the house by nine, although recently my schedule has been somewhat interrupted.'

Amber stared up at him, wanting him to leave and yet reluctant to be abandoned in a strange house.

'Something wrong?' he enquired dulcetly, watching the shadows chase across her golden eyes. 'Or are you waiting for me to seal our bargain in the traditional manner?'

It was several seconds before Amber realised what he meant, and she cringed inwardly wondering if he thought she had been mutely hoping that he would kiss her.

'Certainly not,' she told him with as much cool composure as she could muster. 'You're buying my time, not my body.'

His suave, 'Perhaps that's just as well,' left a bitter aftertaste long after he himself had gone, reminding her yet again that she was no longer a girl men would want to hold in their arms or kiss. For several totally irresponsible seconds she allowed herself to wonder what it would be like to be kissed by Joel Sinclair. His kisses wouldn't be like Rob's, she thought instinctively; there would be nothing tentative or rushed about them. He would know exactly how to arouse a woman's desire; how to fan it until it threatened to become a raging inferno. Horrified by the train of her thoughts, she started to undress, realising almost too late that she had nothing to wear. Shrugging wearily, she decided that she was too tired to care whether she slept in a nightdress or the nude. Fortunately the bathroom, unlike the bedroom, was adequately heated, and she was able to wash out her undies and tights and place them on the hot towel rail to dry ready for the morning.

CHAPTER TWO

IT was the sound of a child crying that eventually roused Amber. She sat up in bed, listening in the darkness preceding dawn, and stretched her ears for the sound which had disturbed her slumbers. It came again—bitterly hopeless sobs; not the normal cry of a young child, and strangely moved, she slid out of bed, intent on discovering what was happening.

She was halfway across the room before she remembered she had no robe. The bathroom afforded a huge bathsheet which she wrapped sarong-wise around her too thin body, before opening her bedroom door.

It wasn't hard to find Paul's room; but what did surprise Amber when she opened the door was that the little boy was all alone, curled up in a small foetal ball in the middle of a rumpled heap of bedclothes.

'Paul.' She whispered his name, and had the satisfaction of seeing his tears stop as he registered her presence.

'Who are you?' The words were wrung from him between sobs.

Amber walked awkwardly towards the bed and switched on the lamp, her breath catching in her throat as she saw the small boy's features properly for the first time. He was a perfect miniature replica of his father!

'My name's Amber.' she answered matter-of-factly. 'Who are you?'

'I'm Paul Sinclair, and this is my daddy's house.'

'Were you having a bad dream?' Amber asked him conversationally.

The small face closed up. 'Sort of.' The reply was deliberately uncommunicative.

'Horrid, aren't they?' Amber sympathised, pretending she had not noticed his withdrawal. 'Would you like me to get you a glass of milk?'

'I'm not thirsty. What are you doing here?'

'Your daddy brought me,' Amber explained, starting to smooth the crumpled sheets. As she did so, she accidentally revealed the thin child's body, dressed in over-large pyjamas which had ridden up to reveal a scarred and very frail-looking leg.

She could feel Paul going rigid when he knew she was looking at him, and her heart went out to the small child. She knew exactly what he was feeling. A thought suddenly struck her. Was this one of the reasons why Joel Sinclair wanted to marry her, because he thought she would have something in common with his son? But no; he had stipulated that their marriage was only to last six months, and besides, he didn't strike her as the kind of man who would marry simply because of emotion.

Paul had turned away from her and was lying rigidly in the bed, his stiff little back expressive of all she herself had felt and never been able to say. She could almost feel him wishing her away.

She touched his arm gently. 'Paul . . . You don't have to hide your leg away from me, you know.'

If anything the little boy became even more stiff.

'Look,' she said lightly, 'my leg's the same.'

At first he didn't move, and then very slowly

and disbelievingly he turned towards her.

'Let me see it.'

Obligingly she raised the hem of the bathsheet, holding her breath as she waited for Paul's reaction. For some obscure reason it had become overwhelmingly important that she win the confidence of this withdrawn, too thin and pale child. Perhaps it was an innate fellow-feeling that told her that he had been fibbed to and fobbed off too often to accept platitudes any longer, and for the first time since her accident she actually didn't mind someone seeing the unpleasant scars.

Even when Paul's small stubby fingers touched the ridged and puckered skin she didn't flinch.

'I was knocked down by a car— how did you get yours?' she asked conversationally.

'He was in a car accident—with his mother,' drawled a mocking familiar voice from the doorway.

Shock jolted through Amber as she saw Joel's lean frame propped up against the door, the brief terry towelling robe he was wearing doing nothing to conceal the potent masculinity of his body. As though it were a magnet it drew Amber's fevered gaze, hot pulses beating insistently through her veins in mute reaction to the sensuality of the lean-muscled male body. What was happening to her? She had never felt like this with Rob. Was it something to do with the fact that she now knew that there would be no lover, no fulfilment for her? Was that what was making her so intensely aware of Joel Sinclair; a stranger?

'Oh, don't look like that,' Joel drawled, totally misunderstanding the reason for her shocked expression. 'She got off completely unscathed.

You ought to be asleep,' he told his son, walking across to the bed, which depressed under his weight.

'I heard him crying,' Amber explained the reason for her presence.

'And like the compassionate motherly creature that you are you came to investigate.'

'Her name's Amber,' Paul told his father, suddenly joining in the conversation. 'And her leg is like mine.'

Over his head golden eyes met grey, and Amber knew that in some part she had been right, unbelievable though it seemed, and that Joel Sinclair had made her that offer of a temporary marriage because of his son's damaged leg.

'Are you going to stay with us?' he demanded suddenly of Amber, adding to Joel, 'I like her, Daddy—make her stay. I don't want her to go away like Mummy did.' Tears filled his eyes, and Amber's tender heart was wrung with pity. Why wasn't this child with his mother, wherever she was? It was obvious from what Joel had said that he wasn't a widower, so where was his wife? Obviously she couldn't ask in front of Paul.

'I won't, Paul,' Joel assured him softly. 'Amber is going to come and live with us for a while.'

'Will she be my new mummy?'

The air was fraught with sudden tension. Amber could feel it in the sudden tensing of Joel's body, the watchful expression in his eyes.

'We'll see, Paul. Now try to go back to sleep.'

'I want Amber to kiss me first,' Paul protested, turning towards her.

Amber's own eyes were damp as she leaned down to kiss the soft childish skin. Paul put his arms round her neck, hugging her fiercely, and it was Joel who released the small clinging fingers and switched off the bedside light.

'Perhaps I ought to stay with him until he falls asleep,' Amber suggested in a soft whisper. There was a chair beside the bed, and she would be quite happy to sit in it until Paul drifted off.

'If you're sure you don't mind? I didn't get back until the early hours.'

It was very peaceful, listening to the gradually deepening sounds of Paul's breathing, going over what she had just learned. Poor Paul! The accident must have been a traumatic experience for him; doubly so because his mother had been with him at the time. And what of her? How she must have suffered, Amber reflected, especially if she had been driving. She must ask Joel how seriously damaged Paul's leg was. Slowly her own eyes started to close, and when dawn finally tinged the sky Amber herself was too deeply asleep to see it.

The warm male fingers on her shoulder felt vaguely familiar. Submerged in dreams, she murmured Rob's name, rubbing her face against the male hand, a slight smile curving the soft warmth of her mouth.

'Darling ...' The word left her lips of a faint sigh, her eyes opening, golden with happiness and love, trust in the shyly provocative manner in which she raised her face for Rob's kiss.

Only there was no Rob any longer, but the knowledge came too late to stop the swift downward descent of a dark male head, predatory lips capturing the softness of her own in a kiss that tingled warmly right through her body to her toes, bringing it fully alive for the first time in months.

Joel's hands gripped the slenderness of her body beneath her arms, and hauled her effortlessly out of the chair.

'Well, well!'

Fully awake, Amber saw the dangerous glitter in the grey eyes she had previously thought of as cold. Now they were hot, burning with an anger that threatened to destroy everything in its path.

'And just who is Rob?'

'He was my fiancé.' When she had told him about her accident and her mother's remarriage, Amber had omitted to mention Rob and their now defunct engagement.

'Rob?' The razor-sharp word warned her that she was treading treacherous ground.

'We were engaged,' she told him. 'He's a doctor, but he wants to specialise, and specialists can't afford invalid wives.'

'So he ditched you?' he asked crisply.

Stung, Amber retorted, 'What makes you think that?'

'If he hadn't, you wouldn't be dreaming about him the way you were. Don't ever mistake me for another man again, Amber, and just to make sure you won't . . .'

She could feel the palms of his hands resting against the gentle swell of her breasts and her heart started to thunder in panic, but there was no avoiding those punishing lips, bent on exacting revenge for her mistake, and teaching her that he was most definitely not Rob. Rob had never kissed her like this, with a cool skill that demanded contempt, but which instead brought from her trembling lips a response that astounded her in its intensity. She tried to pull away, and felt her bathsheet begin to slip, her face crimsoning as she realised that Joel was gazing with frank enjoyment as the swelling femininity of her breasts.

'I take it there's no chance of a reconciliation with this Rob?' he questioned softly as Amber secured her towel.

She shook her head.

'No, and even if there was I wouldn't want one.'

'You're after bigger game now, is that it? A struggling physician is no longer your beau ideal?'

In his bed Paul stirred, and Joel frowned. 'I came to tell you it's nearly eight. Let Paul sleep on this morning. I want to talk to you before I leave for Kendal.'

'I'll be downstairs in half an hour,' she promised curtly.

In her own room, dressing in the same clothes she had worn the previous day she tried not to remember how she had felt when Joel kissed her. Since Rob had left her she had been driven by one ambition and one only: to recover her old mobility and then confront him with all that he had thrown away when he had turned his back on her love because she was no longer the whole, unharmed girl she had been before this accident.

This compulsion had been the only thing that had kept her going; the only reason she had even considered Joel Sinclair's outrageous suggestion, and yet now she was experiencing another emotion—compassion for Paul, a child who was obviously suffering as much as she was herself. poor little boy. Why wasn't his mother with him?

Perhaps if she stopped dawdling in her room and went down for breakfast she might find out, she told herself briskly. In the bright morning light her clothes looked dowdy and dull, and just for a moment she regretted the new, pretty things she had bought for the holiday she and Rob had planned, but that moment was swiftly banished, and the fierce light of battle entered her eyes as she remembered how Joel Sinclair had looked at her and kissed her. She wanted the twenty-five thousand pounds he was offering her badly enough to accept his proposition, but she fully intended to make it absolutely clear to him that their marriage would be a business arrangement only, a big step along the road to achieving her ultimate goal; although he was not to know that. The way in which she intended to spend the money he paid her was nothing to do with Joel Sinclair.

She found him in a large, beautifully modernised kitchen with dark oak units and a mellow tiled floor. To Amber's amazement he was standing by a hob frying bacon, the rich aroma filling the room. Nearby coffee percolated, and the table had been set for breakfast, with grapefruit in two bowls and cereal in the third.

'What's the matter?' Joel enquired in amusement when she came to an abrupt halt just inside the door. 'Surprised to discover I know how to fend for myself? It's one of the first rules of survival, although I admit I'm no Cordon Bleu. Besides, a father bringing up a child alone needs to know at least the rudiments of running a home. I'm fortunate in having Mrs Downs, but in the eyes of divorce judges, housekeepers aren't particularly adequate substitutes for mothers, which is why I need to furnish myself with a wife—albeit on a temporary basis. Hungry?' he asked, indicating the pan of sizzling bacon and reaching across for some large brown eggs. On the point of shaking her head, Amber suddenly changed her mind. She had had next to nothing to eat yesterday, or for several days come to that, and the bacon did smell tantalisingly appetising.

'A little,' she admitted, surprised that she had lowered her guard for long enough to make the admission. 'Shall I wake Paul?'

'No, let him sleep. It will be easier for us to talk without him here. You can see what a dangerously vulnerable emotional state he's in—a result of a combination of things; his accident and losing his mother mainly.'

It was significant that Joel put Paul's accident first, Amber thought. He was too hard a man to fully appreciate the effect losing his mother would have on a small child—or to admit perhaps that he might himself be in some way to blame for Paul's vulnerability.

'Yes,' she agreed. 'He seems to have similar injuries to mine.'

'Which is one of the reasons I put the proposal I did to you.'

'I guessed,' Amber supplied wryly. 'Have the doctors given you any indication as to how bad it will be?'

Joel shrugged. 'They're reluctant to commit themselves at this stage—understandably. Paul's case is complicated by the fact that at the same time as he received his injuries he underwent severe emotional trauma. I've already said that he was with his mother at the time. What I didn't tell you—couldn't tell you while he was there—was that she was on her way to see her lover and intended to leave Paul with her friend for the afternoon. They say those most closely involved are always the last to know—a cliché, but true in my case. I had no idea. Oh, I knew there was something, Teri had made that much perfectly plain—I even suspected there were . . . diversions, but not that one of them was serious enough to make her put her child's life at risk so that she could be with her lover. He was an American working on the North Sea oilrigs whom she met while he was on holiday here. As the son of a Texan oil millionaire he had a super-abundance of the quality that appeals most to Teri in men—money—a trait she apparently shares with you,' he added cynically. 'Which is one of the reasons I decided to put my suggestion to you. A woman who can be bought for a few paltry thousand pounds isn't going to allow emotion to cloud issues at a later stage. This marriage is most definitely only of a temporary nature—I didn't want someone who might get the wrong idea and want to make things permanent.'

There was no reason why his words should be like a splash of icy water, and certainly in the circumstances Amber had no right to feel mortally affronted both by his cynical observation and being classed with Paul's mother, and yet for some obscure reason she did.

'Where is Paul's mother now?' she asked curiously, recoiling a little from the heaped plate of bacon and eggs he put in front of her.

'Eat it while it's hot,' he admonished, putting another plate on the table and pulling up a chair to sit down opposite her. 'Paul's mother? As far as I know she's living in bliss and the lap of luxury as

Mrs Hal Bryden the Fourth, somewhere in the good ole U.S. of A.'

'She divorced you?'

Joel shook his head, his eyes hardening to a flinty grey. 'I divorced her—not because she was unfaithful—I'm not naïve enough to think he was the first. No, I divorced her because of Paul. She'd risked his life once for her own pleasure, I wasn't about to let it happen again. I asked for custody and got it—now she's contesting the judge's decision, claiming that although at the time of the divorce she wasn't able to offer Paul a stable family background, now that she has remarried she's more able to claim full custody. My solicitor believes she has grounds for a good and plausible case, and because I can't afford to take any more risks with Paul's life, I'm determined not to give her the slightest opportunity of changing the judge's decision; and that means being able to provide him with as much of a family background as she can—a father and a mother!'

'But you said you only wanted to be married for six months?' Amber protested.

'The longer I have sole custody of Paul without any problems the less likely a judge is to reverse his decision. I know Teri; patience was never her strong suit. Within six months she'll be ready to admit defeat.'

'And Paul?' Amber asked, suddenly angry on the little boy's behalf. 'Has anyone consulted him? Has he been asked whether or not he wants to stay with you?'

'No,' Joel told her evenly, 'and for the simple reason that ever since the accident he has never once—until last night—mentioned his mother. In point of fact he didn't see much of her before the divorce. Teri spent a good deal of time in the States with her family, and she always refused to take Paul, claiming that he was too young to travel. Too young to travel, but not too young to send away to school, or so she was trying to persuade me. Oh, I'm not trying to put all the blame on her. I was equally neglectful,' Joel admitted. 'My business takes me away a good deal, and weeks would go by with me only seeing Paul for the odd half hour when he was in bed. It took the accident to show me what was happening; how I was missing out on my son's formative years, depriving him of the love and affection which as my son he had a right to expect from me. In time, with care and a stable background, he should outgrow the trauma of what happened—he was trapped in the back of the car when it crashed. Teri always drove far too fast. She left him alone when she ran back to the telephone kiosk she'd passed to ring her lover and warn him not to expect her, and the poor kid must have thought she'd deserted him for good. He was hysterical by the time the doctor got to him, and in trying to pull himself free had worsened the injury to his leg.'

Amber was appalled, sickened by the crass selfishness of Paul's mother. How could any mother desert her child at a moment like that?

'The doctors believe that once the emotional scars start to heal his leg will respond better to treatment, but another emotional upheaval like being suddenly forced to go and live with Teri could set him back years.'

Amber could well understand Joel's dilemma.

'I'm hoping to persuade an aunt of mine, who at

present lives in Australia to make her home with us and act as a surrogate mother to Paul, someone he can come to rely on and trust. He never trusted Teri; she was too changeable, her moods too violent for him to know where he was with her. She never wanted a child; Paul's conception was a mistake. In more ways than one,' he added under his breath. 'Once she knows I've remarried, Teri will do everything she can to try and get the court to revoke their decision in her favour, and for that reason, to the outside world at least, our marriage must be seen to be completely normal. Her husband is an extremely rich man; rich enough for Teri to be able to hire private detectives to spy on us in public. Inside this house, when we're alone, we can live as strangers, but to the rest of the world you must be a girl I've fallen deeply in love with and who loves me in return. You will share my bedroom and my bed.' He saw Amber's expression and raised a mocking eyebrow. 'Something wrong?'

Amber forced herself to meet his glance squarely, reminding herself how desperately she needed his money.

'Our marriage will be strictly a business arrangement?'

'By which I take it that you mean no sex?' Joel countered coolly. 'But of course. I thought I'd made that plain; even if you were Venus herself you'd be perfectly safe. Mercenary women have no appeal for me—in fact I find them a complete turn-off; and your charms . . .' His eyes flicked cruelly over her too thin body and misshapen leg before returning to her paper-white face, 'such as they are, are not sufficient to change my mind. In public we will be newly married lovers; but there's no likelihood of *me* forgetting that it's just a charade. Want to back out?'

The words which would free her from his taunting presence hovered on her lips, but before she could utter them two pictures flashed through her mind. The first, surprisingly, was of Paul, small and vulnerable as he watched her with wary eyes; and the second was of Rob, embarrassed and uncomfortable as he left her hospital bedside for the last time. Together they were powerful enough to bridle her tongue, and taking her silence as a denial, Joel continued smoothly, 'Very well. There's no point in delaying unnecessarily. I'll organise a special licence—it will make our marriage appear all the more romantic; there's something recklessly foolhardy about a man who marries with all the haste implied by a special licence, don't you agree?' Without waiting for her reply he added, 'Oh, there's just one more small detail. Before we do marry I should like you to sign a document I'll have drawn up acknowledging the temporary nature of our marriage and the fact that you're being paid to serve in the capacity of my wife for a brief period. A form of insurance for me just in case you get any silly ideas.'

'You flatter yourself,' Amber gritted at him. 'Hasn't losing one wife to another man taught you anything about the opposite sex?'

She had the satisfaction of seeing the faint flush of anger lying along his cheekbones and leaping to life in the granite eyes, but he had himself under control almost immediately, the anger masked by the cynical expression she was coming to recognise.

'A great deal,' he drawled, 'but millionaires naïve enough to fall for women like you and Teri are thin on the ground, and you might just decide to settle for second best.'

CHAPTER THREE

'EVERYTHING is arranged. I've fixed the ceremony for Tuesday, which gives us the weekend to get organised. First on the agenda, I suspect, will be a shopping trip. You'll need a wedding ring,' Joel informed Amber dryly, 'and new clothes.' His eyes slid assessingly over the plain grey skirt and dull white blouse she had been wearing for her interview, and which were still the only clothes she possessed, after two days in his home, having vetoed her suggestion that she returned to Birmingham to collect her others. There were things she had to do, she protested—her mother to tell; her landlady.

All tasks which which could be attended to by telephone, Joel had reminded her, letting her know that he wasn't going to give her the opportunity to back out of their arrangement.

They were in his study, an attractive masculine room at the back of the house furnished with comfortable leather chairs, a desk, some beautiful reproduction Georgian filing cabinets disguised as bow-fronted chests and bookcases containing a wide variety of books from novels to highly technical literature on computer technology which Amber had learned was the field in which his companies operated.

Tomorrow would be her first test as Joel's fiancée. Mrs Downs, whom Joel had telephoned and asked not to bother to come in the other two days, was due to arrive in the morning. Joel had assured her that she would not find it difficult to keep up the pretence in front of the other woman, but Amber wasn't too sure.

'Worrying about tomorrow?' Joel drawled, accurately reading her mind. 'Don't be. Just think of yourself as an actress hired to play a part, for which you're being paid extremely generously. After that the rest should come naturally. All women are actresses at heart.'

His cynical observation jarred, even though she tried to pretend it left her unmoved. She glanced at her watch. Joel had arrived from Kendal half an hour before and it was now nearly seven.

'It's Paul's bedtime,' she reminded him. 'I promised I'd read to him. Shall I wait until you've seen him?'

'Why don't we both go up together?' Joel suggested. 'That way we can break the happy news to him.'

Amber knew that Joel had been observing Paul's reaction to her—and hers to him—but much as she liked the little boy, she had no intention of encouraging him to become too fond of her. It simply wouldn't be fair either to him or to her. In some way she almost wished he had taken a dislike to her, but she knew beyond any shadow of doubt now that if he had Joel would have instantly abandoned his plans to marry her. Think of the money, she kept reminding herself; the money which was to be the instrument of her eventual revenge against Rob. If she closed her eyes and thought hard enough she could almost conjure up the image of how it would be; of her own unannounced arrival at wherever Rob was, and his astonishment when he saw her restored to full health, walking as gracefully as she had done in the past. She would be beautifully dressed, elegantly made up; and she would have the pleasure of watching him see what he had so callously thrown away.

As always the mental imagery helped to reinforce her determination. Paul wouldn't be hurt, she promised herself. She wouldn't allow that to happen. And Joel? She glanced sideways at him. Any man who could strike the type of bargain he had struck with her and demand written acknowledgement of that bargain wasn't capable of being hurt.

But he must have been once, a tiny inner voice reminded her, otherwise he would never have married Teri in the first place. What was she like? Amber wondered.

'So that's settled,' Joel said suavely, cutting through her thoughts, 'Tomorrow we go to Kendal shopping. Mrs Downs will look after Paul. We'd better make a full day of it—and an evening as well. It will be expected; after all, it isn't every day a man gets engaged.'

Not a woman either, Amber thought sadly, and this would be her first formal engagement. Rob had never given her a ring.

Paul was playing with some toy soldiers when they went up to his room.

He and Amber had grown quite friendly during the two days she had been staying at the house. He accepted her presence as a friend of his father's without comment, but his mother and the life the three of them had shared before his accident were never mentioned. Amber understood. Like him she found the past still too raw a wound to discuss it with others, and perhaps because of their similar injuries a bond seemed to have been formed between them; to such an extent that Paul had begun to talk freely to her about his leg, comparing it to hers and asking her numerous questions about the operations she had undergone. his favourite seemed to be whether Amber would ever get properly better, and recognising it as a plea for assurance that he would get better, she had lied and told him what he wanted to hear.

He asked her again, as she knelt awkwardly to help him pack away the soldiers.

'I expect so,' she lied, determinedly cheerfully, glad of the long sweep of her hair to conceal her expression from Joel.

'Will I?'

This time it was Joel who answered, lifting the little boy up in his arms until the two male faces, so similar in features, were only inches apart. 'Yes, you will, Paul,' he assured him firmly. 'But it won't be easy. You'll have to help—do those exercises Doctor Raines told you about.'

Paul pulled a face.

'I don't like them,' he protested. 'They hurt!'

'Only at first,' Amber felt moved to say, adding to Joel, 'I studied physiotherapy for a few months before I decided on general nursing, if you like I could help Paul with his exercises . . .'

'We could do them together,' Paul suggested, pleased, glancing at Amber's leg. 'Then we'd both get better.'

Amber already knew that exercises would do little to improve her own injured muscles; the only hope of full mobility she had was the American operation which replaced destroyed muscles with fresh tissue grafted from other parts of the body, a lengthy and expensive business; but she didn't want to destroy Paul's optimism, so she smiled and agreed that indeed it would.

'Thanks for reassuring Paul like that,' Joel said when Paul was asleep and they had returned downstairs. 'One of the most difficult problems has been trying to get over his aversion to the exercises he has to do. The problem is he's too young to understand the need for them properly, but Doctor Raines says that without them . . .' he looked closely at Amber. '*Can* you help him with them?'

'I think so. I'll need someone to show me exactly what has to be done.'

'Doctor Raines told me that swimming would help, but there just aren't sufficient facilities locally, otherwise both of you . . .'

'It wouldn't do any good in my case,' Amber began, breaking off as she realised how close she had come to confiding the truth to him.

'Why not?' His eyes sharpened and she felt a prickle of awareness as his eyes slid down her body to the leg she had tucked from habit behind the healthy one.

'I . . . I have to have another operation,' she prevaricated a little wildly, 'in six months' time.'

'But you will recover fully?'

'Oh yes.' Her voice sounded brittle and false even to her own ears. 'Yes, of course.'

'No wonder you accepted my proposition so readily,' Joel said grimly. 'A ready-made comfortable existence until your operation; with the bonus of twenty-five thousand at the end of it.'

'I didn't ask you to pick me,' Amber flared. 'If you want to change your mind . . .'

'Incredible,' Joel muttered under his breath as he shook his head. 'Who would have dreamed anyone so innocent-looking could be so hard?'

If I am it's because that's what your sex made me, Amber longed to scream at him, but the words were suppressed, her face a tight mask as she forced a smile almost as mocking as his own, and reminded him,

'But that's what you wanted, wasn't it? A gold-digger whom you could pay off with a clear conscience and no complications?'

Mrs Downs arrived in the morning just as they were finishing breakfast, a tall gaunt woman with greying hair and a forbidding expression, which belied the smile warming her eyes when Joel introduced her to Amber.

'So it's getting wed the two of you are, is it?' she said forthrightly when Joel had broken the news.

'We are indeed,' Joel confirmed, smiling and slipping a hard arm round Amber's shoulders, drawing her back against the firm warmth of his chest. In other circumstances she would have found something distinctly reassuring about the comfortingly steady thud of his heart, the calm way in which he dealt with Mrs Downs' surprise, the aura of strength and reliability emanating from him and wrapping her in a protective embrace.

'So, and you'll want me to keep an eye on young Paul here while you're off to Kendal?'

'If you wouldn't mind,' Joel agreed courteously. 'I should like to take Amber out to dinner tonight, if you're able to stay with Paul. Everything has happened so quickly we haven't even been able to celebrate our engagement yet.'

The tender look he gave her almost made Amber catch her breath in astonishment; it was so plausibly real. Her eyes widened, and like the skilled master tactician he was Joel was quick to take advantage of the moment, turning her gently towards him and rubbing his thumb provocatively across her parted lips before closing them with a light kiss.

Amber could almost see Mrs Downs' reserve melting and read the other woman's mind. It was obvious that Joel had convinced her that they were deeply in love, and her own wildly flushed cheeks and flustered manner would only serve to reinforce her belief.

Paul regarded them with interest from his chair.

'Why are you kissing Amber?' he questioned curiously.

He had already accepted Joel's information that he and Amber were to marry, but still Amber found herself holding her breath, half expecting the little boy to protest about their intimacy.

'Because she's going to marry me,' Joel replied evenly when Mrs Downs bustled out to remove her coat and outdoor shoes.

'You and Teri were married, but you never kissed her like that,' Paul remarked, startling Amber both by his use of his mother's christian name and what he had said.

'That was different,' was Joel's oblique comment, and Amber sensed from his withdrawn look that he was probably re-living certain intensely private moments of his relationship with his ex-wife; moments to which Paul would not have been privy. A kind of dull sickness took possession of her, and as she struggled to fight it off she heard Mrs Downs returning.

'Time we were on our way,' Joel said coolly, grasping Amber's arm. 'Be a good boy for Mrs Downs, Paul.'

'If I am, will you bring me a present?' he asked appealingly.

'Maybe.' Joel was stern, and Amber knew instinctively that he would make a good father, loving, but firm.

The car was parked outside the house, which Amber had now discovered overlooked the lake they had passed on the night Joel had first brought her to his house. Landscaped gardens swept down to the lakeside where a motorboat was moored, behind the house rose the fells, thickly forested, protecting the house from the worst of the northern elements. Today the sky was grey and overcast; an icy wind blowing which seemed to go straight through Amber's thin city coat. She stumbled as she tried to negotiate the gravelled drive, and Joel's hand came out to support her instantly. She ignored it, flushing to the roots of her hair and assiduously avoiding him as she fought to regain her balance, only to lose it again a minute later.

'You know what they say about pride,' came Joel's voice somewhere in the region of her left ear as he caught her deftly. 'It always goes before a fall. There's no shame in what's happened to you, Amber; you sometimes behave as though being a little awkward in your movements is blood brother to leprosy!'

Amber was still seething over the words 'a little awkward,' when he scooped her up and deposited her none too gently in the front passenger seat of the XJ10, closing the door very firmly on her before walking round to the driver's door and sliding in beside her.

The car smelled richly of expensive hide; and just the faintest echo of the clean masculine fragrance Joel wore. Watching his fluid movements as he set the car in motion, the powerful thigh muscles contracting visibly beneath the fine wool of his suit, Amber felt her own eyes going to her scarred leg.

'Why are you so obsessed by your injury?' Joel demanded, shocking her with the realisation that he had noticed and correctly interpreted her look.

'Perhaps because it's brought home to me the fact that if you're a woman, and physically imperfect in some way, it doesn't matter how intelligent or caring you are, you're judged and found wanting on the evidence of physical disability.'

'Which only goes to show that you're on the wrong road in life; or haven't you realised yet that when you adopt money as your one god, your reason for living, you say goodbye to compassion, respect, and the sort of men who look beneath the surface to find out what sort of woman lives under the skin. Men who exchange their wealth for a woman are buying a status symbol and they expect it to be as perfect as a masterpiece, an art treasure or a piece of antique furniture. If you make it known that you're on sale, you can't blame the buyers for rejecting you as faulty goods—a reject,' he finished cruelly.

After that Amber sat in white-faced pain as they drove along the lake side and then up, out of the valley, through scenery so peaceful and beautiful that it would have been balm to any soul less wounded than hers.

In the autumn these hills would be a living mass of rich colour, she thought absently, studying the fresh spring green of the ferns growing by the water's edge, and the new leaves just unfurling from their sticky protective covering.

Kendal was busy, but Joel found a parking space without too much difficulty, outside the office block which housed his company's offices. The block was new, well designed to blend in with its surroundings, and Amber felt the first stirrings of curiosity about what went on behind the closed doors of the offices. Joel had told her very little about his business affairs apart from the fact that they concerned computer technology. She stole a quick glance at his shuttered profile as he helped her out of the car. The thrusting jaw and square chin belonged to a man who knew where he wanted to go and was determined enough to get there, the cool grey eyes said that he would not be pressured into making rash decsions, while the curling mouth hinted intriguingly at a sexuality which, while not blatant, was a very powerful force nonetheless. He was a man who was intensely male; sure of himself and his masculinity without in any way being brash of overtly macho. There was pride, and unconscious male arrogance, in the way he moved, with all the lithe muscularity of someone born to conquer, both in his personal and business life. Which made it all the harder to understand why Teri had sought diversion else-where. Something deep and instinctive within her warned Amber that in Joel's arms a woman could come dangerously close to forgetting everything but the heady pleasure of just being there; of willingly exchanging the shadowy promised future for the heady reality of the present.

Deep in thought, she hadn't realised that they had reached the town centre. Joel made unerringly for a discreetly expensive jewellers, whose windows were adorned with precious metals and stones that made Amber catch her breath in purely feminine pleasure.

Inside a salesman stepped forward; Joel murmured something Amber couldn't hear and the next moment they were being ushered discreetly into a small adjoining room comfortably furnished with deep padded wicker chairs, a selection of rings swiftly produced for their inspection.

As well as the more traditional rings, the jewellers specialised in an exclusive range of modern engagement rings with matching wedding rings. One of these in particular caught Amber's eye, as much for its unusual design as for its elegant simplicity. Two interlocking rings comprising three differing shades of gold were displayed on a bed of black velvet, diamonds sparkling brightly in one of them.

'Ah yes,' the salesman enthused, noticing Amber's interest. 'Those are rather special. The diamonds are excellent quality, and the rings themselves were designed specifically for them. Would you care to try them?'

Amber started to shake her head, knowing instinctively that the rings would be frighteningly expensive, but to her dismay Joel overruled her by the simple expedient of picking up the rings and sliding them one after the other on to her shaking finger. They fitted perfectly, the delicate shape flattering her slender hand.

'We'll take them,' Joel told the salesman decisively, ignoring Amber's protests. 'And my wife would like some earrings as well. Something plain and simple—diamonds, I think.'

Again Amber tried to protest, but when the salesman had disappeared to bring some earrings to show her, Joel leaned across and said coolly, 'As my wife you will be expected to wear some jewellery. Teri was particularly addicted to it, and I don't want people saying I can't afford to supply you with the same perks she enjoyed.'

She might have known, Amber thought wretchedly, all her pleasure in the flashing stones the salesman produced negated by the knowledge that they were not so much a gift but more of a publicity exercise, designed to convince the world of a love that did not exist.

She picked the smallest stones she could, but once again Joel overruled her, choosing with an unerring eye for style and quality another pair, far larger, and to judge from the salesman's pleased expression, more expensive.

Amber had expected Joel to insist on her wearing the engagement ring straight away, but when she went to pick it up, he stopped her, grasping her wrist and scooping up the band of gold.

'Clothes now,' he told her when they emerged from the jewellers, adding sardonically, 'Try to look as though you're enjoying yourself—if nothing else helps try reminding yourself that you're spending my money. It never failed with Teri.'

'But I'm not Teri,' Amber snapped, colouring when she saw the way he looked at her.

'No,' he agreed slowly, 'you're not.'

The words seemed to hang on the air, waiting for the rider that didn't come—that Joel regretted the omission. Was he still in love with his ex-wife? Amber wondered. She shrugged the thought aside, telling herself that Joel's feelings were no concern of hers.

'In here.' He touched her arm lightly, propelling her into a small boutique of the type Amber normally walked past enviously, ignoring the lure of the one or two outrageously expensive garments in their windows.

The shop was empty apart from the saleswoman, who came forward with a pleasant smile.

'My fiancée needs some new clothes,' Joel told her with an unexpectedly charming smile. 'She's been ill recently and has lost weight. We're getting married in three days' time, and she keeps insisting on telling me that she simply can't put together a new wardrobe in that time.'

Very obviously rising to the challenge, the saleswoman bustled importantly about the cool gold and white interior of the boutique, clicking her tongue over Amber's slender frame, and exclaiming over her fragile appearance, while tactfully ignoring the appearance of her leg.

'This could take some time,' she told Joel with a smile. 'If you have any other shopping to do . . .'

Taking the hint, Joel glanced at his watch and told Amber he would return for her in an hour. 'And remember,' he warned her, bestowing another of his mock tender smiles, 'I want you to dress like the woman I love!'

The warning was so subtly couched that only Amber was aware of it, Joel's departure leaving the saleswoman beaming fatuously.

'Aren't you the lucky one?' she exclaimed. 'When did he say you were getting married?'

'Monday,' Amber told her, hoping her voice didn't sound as hollow as it felt.

Had anyone told her that she could completely refurbish her wardrobe in an hour she would have laughed at them, but with the saleswoman's skilled assistance it didn't prove to be an impossibility after all.

There was a cream suit with a belted jacket and a delicate self-embroidery on the lapels and the skirt just above the elegant fan of pleats. Amber wanted to buy a blouse to wear under the jacket, but the saleswoman said that to do so would spoil the line of the suit.

A cocktail dress in a matt black jersey with tiny shoestring straps and a glittering matador-shaped jacket fitted her like a second skin and did something unexpected to the pale translucency of skin Amber had privately thought insipid beforehand. An entrancing range of separates in a clear fashionable blue were added to the growing pile; a silk dress in dark gold with a flattering draped neckline and a slender skirt was pronounced a 'must', and in a final reckless moment of abandon Amber fell for a slim blouson in pale cream suede with gathered cuffs.

Joel returned exactly an hour after he had left, just as the saleswoman was persuading her to try a spectacular picture hat in soft cream trimmed with artificial flowers.

'We'll take it,' he announced decisively, watching her. 'And that.' He gestured to a dress hanging on the rail which Amber had discarded as far too expensive. It was a model, Edwardian in conception, in a soft shade of peach lace with a deeply plunging neckline and a lace choker ornamented with peach silk flowers. Amber had tried the dress, fallen in love with it, and regretfully put it on one side, as much for the fact that she thought it totally unsuited to her as the price.

As they left the shop the saleswoman recommended a beauty salon where Amber could have her face made up and her hair done.

'Later,' Joel told her as he grasped the expensively embossed black and gold carriers. 'First, some lunch.'

They ate in the restaurant of a comfortable hotel where the food was good without being pretentious and Amber was able to relax and feel at ease, without feeling she was the cynosure of all eyes in her dull clothes. Dismissing the idea that Joel had deliberately chosen the restaurant to spare her any embarrassment, she reminded herself that everything she was doing now was only a prelude to what would happen once she had his twenty-five thousand pounds.

After lunch Joel suggested that while she was visiting the hairdresser he would call at his office.

'After all,' he reminded her with an ironic smile, 'I won't have much opportunity to work on Monday!'

The hair-stylist enthused over the texture and colour of Amber's hair, snipping very little off the length but re-shaping it so that it hung in a shiny fall over her shoulders.

The make-up artist was a pleasant girl who showed her several tricks for emphasising the size and colour of her eyes, and by the time she was ready to leave their experienced and skilled hands Amber was longing to discard her drab interview clothes and change into some of the new things Joel had bought for her. It was so long since she had taken any pleasure in what she wore that the feeling was almost unfamiliar.

After Rob had left her, she had packed away all the new things she had bought for their holiday unworn. She had asked her landlady to send her things on, but she knew that no matter how attractive the things she had bought they simply didn't compare with the clothes Joel had bought for her today.

He was waiting outside the hairdresser's for her in the car, his eyes moving slowly over her shining hair and newly made up face.

'Good,' he said at last. 'I like to know I'm getting value for my money.'

It was like a slap in the face. Amber could feel her newly found confidence draining away as she slid into the car. They had gone several miles before she realised that they were heading away from Joel's home, and as though he read her mind he said calmly,

'We're supposed to be having dinner together, remember? So I thought we'd kill two birds with one stone. There's a hotel not far from here where they hold dinner-dances most Saturdays. I've booked us a room and a table—the room is so that you can change,' he told her acidly, seeing her expression. 'We could well meet some of my friends . . .'

'And you don't want to be ashamed of me?' Amber finished bitterly for him.

'We're supposed to have fallen in love,' Joel pointed out calmly. 'I've yet to meet any woman in love who celebrates that fact dressed like a schoolgirl, and a particularly frumpish one at that.'

Amber was forced to acknowledge the truth of his statement, much as it rankled.

'Neither do I want my friends to think I'm getting married in some hole-and-corner fashion, or that I'm ashamed of my bride,' Joel continued smoothly. 'That isn't the object of the exercise at all. Remember what I told you—no loopholes; no flaws; this marriage is going to be watertight as far as the outside world is concerned.'

The hotel he took her to was several miles outside Kendal, a gracious ivy-clad building with excellent views of the Lakeland peaks. He had booked them adjoining rooms, and there would be plenty of time for Amber to explore the hotel and its environs before they needed to change for dinner, he told her in response to her comment that the hotel grounds looked particularly attractive.

Amber's room overlooked the side of the hotel, and had excellent views of the hills. While she was admiring them a porter came in with her parcels which she directed him to leave on the bed. She had barely started to walk towards them when she heard a brisk tap on the door. Opening it, she found Joel standing outside.

'May I come in?' Without waiting for an answer he walked into her room, glancing assessingly over the extremely comfortable room. 'It just dawned on me that you might decide to explore the grounds alone, and I thought I'd better remind you that we're supposed to be a couple on the brink of engagement, so it might be as well if we were to share the pleasure of their seclusion.'

His glance fell on the bed and the parcels lying there and he walked across to them.

'Have you anything here suitable for walking in?'

Amber thought about the attractive separates she had just bought, and although she was tempted to say that she considered the clothes she was already wearing more than adequate for walking, some perverse streak of femininity she had thought suppressed by her accident surfaced, revolting at the thought of continuing to wear the drab garments she had on when much more attractive clothes were there to be worn.

She was about to reply in the affirmative when her eye was caught by a gold and white box she didn't recognise as being one of her purchases, and she went towards it in dismay, thinking that the porter must have brought it up with her things in error.

'Ah,' Joel drawled, grasping the box, 'a gift for my bride-to-be . . .' He handed it to her, watching her speculatively. 'Aren't you going to open it?'

'You've bought me so much already,' Amber protested, but Joel shrugged her protest aside.

'Props,' he told her laconically. 'A very necessary part of our charade if it's to be played successfully.'

Amber didn't answer, she couldn't. She was too busy staring at the contents of the gold and white box, a terrible anguished pain tearing at her heart as she gazed disbelievingly at the froth of silk, chiffon and lace. Her trembling fingers moved awkwardly over the fragile, cobwebby garments—a nightdress in finest crêpe-de-chine, a matching negligee, delicate, feminine underwear, designed to be worn by a woman confident of her own beauty and her body's ability to reflect that beauty when clad only in brief wisps of satin and lace.

'Something wrong?' Joel enquired dulcetly, watching the play of emotions across her face.

'I can't wear them,' she told him bitterly. 'Please take them away.'

'What's wrong? Aren't they the right size?' His eyes rested provocatively on the soft thrust of her breasts and Amber flushed, knowing as she did that he had judged her measurements almost exactly.

'I can't wear them,' she insisted, turning away from him to add in a low voice, 'You'll have to be content with transforming my public image; or were you hoping that by dressing me in fine silks and satins you could pretend I was Teri?'

Only her anguish could have forced her to say such a foolhardy thing, and she knew she had gone too far the moment she saw the brooding anger in Joel's eyes.

'That would be impossible,' he told her curtly. 'She was a woman who delighted in the sensuality of her body—but then she had good reason to,' he added cruelly, turning on his heel. He paused at the door to say curtly, 'If you want to walk in the grounds I'll meet you downstairs in half an hour.'

Amber shook her head. 'I don't think I'll bother,' she told him tightly, waiting until she was quite, quite sure that he had gone, before flinging herself full length on the bed and crying until there were no more tears left.

What on earth was the matter with her? she asked herself when the storm had finally abated. What did it matter if Joel Sinclair compared her unfavourably with his ex-wife? Why should she care if he insulted her by buying her the kind of frivolous, sensual underwear that he must know mocked and underlined her scarred and disfigured body?

CHAPTER FOUR

To judge by the number of people who had approached their table during the half an hour they had been sitting there, Joel had a good many acquaintances in the locality, Amber reflected, knowing that she was the cynosure of most of the feminine eyes in the room—eyes which had widened slightly, betraying their owners' astonishment as Joel had introduced her as his fiancée; glances which had made her writhe selfconsciously, knowing what a contrast she must present to the other women. Automatically she tucked her damaged leg under their table.

'Something wrong with your steak?' When she shook her head, Joel said softly, 'Then try to look as though you're enjoying it. We're celebrating our engagement—remember?'

As he spoke he leaned forward, capturing one restless hand and conveying her fingers to his lips, kissing the finger bearing his engagement ring lingeringly.

Colour scorched Amber's face. She tried to pull away, gasping as his fingers tightened, knowing that they were being watched.

'That's better,' Joel approved. 'A little colour in your cheeks suits you, you're too pale—and too thin,' he added critically.

'Illness does that to you,' Amber said bitterly. 'I'm sorry if I don't match up to your exacting standards.'

'Beggars can't be choosers,' Joel replied indifferently, 'and you suit my purposes well enough.'

He had ordered champagne, but Amber barely touched the bubbling liquid in her glass. Every now and again her eyes went to the engagement ring he had placed on her finger, a curious little pain twisting her heart. What was the matter with her? It was stupid to feel so ridiculously sentimental over the bestowing of a ring. The ring was just another part of their business arrangement—nothing more.

In an alcove at the far end of the room, musicians struck up a waltz, and couples who had finished their meal got up to dance. Amber watched them, unaware of the wistful expression in her eyes.

'Shall we join them?'

She looked at Joel as though he had struck her.

'Now what's the matter?'

'I'm a cripple,' she reminded him bitterly. 'I can't dance.'

'Can't—or won't?'

Her face as white as the tablecloth, Amber stared at him.

'Have you ever tried?' Joel continued remorselessly. Before Amber could prevent him, he was on his feet, coming round to her side of the table, his fingers burning through the thin silk of her new dress as he urged her to her feet. Caught off guard, Amber stumbled against him, prevented from falling by the hardness of his arm round her waist, drawing her against him in a parody of a lover's embrace.

Once on the dance floor it wasn't as bad as she had dreaded. The lights had been dimmed and the pace of the waltz was slow enough to accommodate her stiff muscles. Pain ached and flared through her calf and she bit down hard on her lip, refusing to give in to the temptation to favour her good leg.

Pain brought a misting of tears to her eyes, which she tried to blink away, knowing that people were watching them.

The dance seemed to go on for ever, and when it eventually ended Amber's whole body was trembling with exhaustion and reaction. As the lights came on Joel's arm slid round her waist, catching her off guard as he pulled her firmly against him, her trembling legs supported by the solid-columned muscle of his. She felt the warmth of his breath grazing her forehead, and lifted her face to tell him to release her, ashamed of the momentary weakness that had made the strength of his body a welcome resting-place, her eyes widening as she read the purpose in his eyes, her mouth parting on a soft protest which was silenced by the firm pressure of his lips.

Amber was no naïve, impressionable teenager. She had been kissed before, and not just by Rob, but never once had she experienced the mind-reeling skill of a kiss that swept aside conventions and reached deep down to the vulnerable core of her, dragging from her throbbing lips a response that shocked and bewildered her.

When Joel lifted his head she couldn't meet his eyes. His drawled, 'Well, you're an excellent actress if nothing else,' left her feeling raw with pain. 'A very convincing demonstration of desire,' he continued harshly, and something in the cold words made Amber look up at him. His eyes were grey lakes of winter ice, rimmed with contempt—

and for what? she raged inwardly. He was the one who had kissed her, who had decided upon this ridiculous charade.

'If you've changed your mind——' she began hesitatingly, only to have her words silenced by the angry oath that ripped from his throat, his face dark with an anger surely totally out of proportion to whatever sin she was supposed to have committed.

'What are you trying to do?' he demanded savagely. 'Up your price? No way! We've made a bargain and you're going to stick to it. Teri bled me dry; and going through that once is enough for any man. And don't even think of running out on me now, Amber,' he threatened softly, 'otherwise a badly scarred leg will be the least of your problems!'

Too terrified to protest, Amber let him bundle her out into the car, aware as he hurried her past the other diners of their amused and speculative glances. She overheard one woman saying quite clearly to her companion, 'I never had Joel down as the impetuous lover, more the cool calm collected type, but he certainly seemed anxious to have his little fiancée all to himself. Why, do you suppose? Surely not an excess of celibacy? I could name at least half a dozen women who'd be more than glad to share his bed.'

As Joel hustled her away, Amber just caught the first angrily muttered words of her male companion's response, his, 'Yourself included, Delia,' heightening her own flush of chagrin. She glanced at Joel's impassive features, but there was no clue to be read there indicating either that he had overheard the woman's comment, or that it was true.

Two days later they were married—a simple church ceremony made possible by the special licence Joel had procured and a broadminded and understanding vicar who seemed to know Joel quite well and obviously did not take exception to his divorced status.

The wedding was a very quiet one—a few friends of Joel's, all strangers to Amber; and Paul, who seemed quite pleased to learn that she was to be his stepmother.

'You're lucky really,' Jennifer Boston, the wife of Joel's accountant, told her over the excellent lunch Joel had arranged at the same hotel where he had taken her dancing two days before. 'Stepchildren can be one of the biggest problems of a second marriage, as I know to my cost.' She grimaced a little, putting out her cigarette with a jerky movement, her face drawn. 'Mike has two, a boy and a girl, and they make my life hell. He has access every other weekend; I look upon those weekends as the penance I have to bear for the pleasure of being Mike's wife. Those two kids hate me, I can tell by the way they look at me, and they never miss an opportunity of talking about their mother; of reminding Mike of things they did together as a family before he and Shirley split up; excluding me. And the damnable thing is that I didn't even meet Mike until he was divorced. God, I shouldn't be telling you all this,' she apologised. 'It must be the champagne—it affects me like that.' She was elegant brunette in her late twenties, plainly in love with her husband, and Amber could see despair in her hazel eyes.

'Perhaps if you and Mike had a child of your own,' she suggested, her eyes straying to where Joel was deep in conversation with Mike and two other guests, also employees of his company.

'I wish to God we could, but Mike won't hear of it. For one thing we can't afford it, or so he says. He still has to support Shirley and the kids— Shirley still has their house—we, on the other hand, have to live in a poky little flat because despite Mike's large salary it's all we can afford. Even some of my salary goes to support Shirley and her children ... Would you believe it, Mike doesn't even trust me not to make sure I don't get pregnant by accident any more ...' She grimaced, and Amber could see tears weren't far away. She beckoned to a hovering waitress and ordered two cups of coffee.

'Heavens, Mike will shoot me for this!' Jennifer exclaimed. 'At least you're not likely to have our problems. Teri's new husband is a very wealthy man. Mike was telling me that she intends to fight a custody battle for Paul—God knows why. She neglected him terribly, you know, poor little mite. I wouldn't be surprised if she's doing it just to spite Joel. In fact I wouldn't be surprised if the whole thing wasn't just some sort of plan to make Joel pay more attention to her. She was like that. Always needling him, always trying to make him jealous. She was obsessively possessive of him; couldn't even bear him to devote time to his business. I don't think for one moment she actually intended to let things go as far as divorce. I'm sure she expected Joel to come running; she must have got the shock of her life when he instituted the proceedings. Poor Joel, he'd had enough. She was a first-rate bitch.'

'Worse than Shirley?' said Amber, trying to lighten the atmosphere.

It drew a reluctant laugh from her companion. 'I do tend to be a little obsessive myself, don't I? In actual fact Shirley isn't such a bitch; more a helpless clinger, if you know what I mean, but Teri . . . She was like a leech, clinging, sucking Joel dry.'

'So there you are, my darling!'

The husky, male voice acted like shock waves on Amber's skin. Jennifer laughed when she flushed, standing up and waving Joel into the chair she had just vacated. 'Something tells me we're decidedly de trop,' she said to her husband.

'I'm a newly married man,' Joel reminded her, giving Amber a long lingering look which rested pointedly on the soft thrust of her breasts beneath the cream silk. 'Can you blame me for getting a little impatient?'

There was a general burst of laughter, and people started to make noises about leaving. Someone asked if they planned to go away on honeymoon, and Amber held her breath, not daring to look at Joel.

'I thought about it,' he murmured to Jennifer. 'But it was impossible to book somewhere secluded enough for long enough; so I'm not taking Amber away until we've been married long enough for me to be willing to share her with other people. I want her all to myself for a very, very long time.'

There was more laughter, while Amber crimsoned, not so much with embarrassment, but more the knowledge that his friends must have thought

Joel had lost his wits, to even mildly desire a girl as deformed as she was.

'You're embarrassing the girl,' Mike Boston protested, adding surprisingly, 'But I think in your shoes, Joel, I'd feel very much the same way. Ready, Paul?'

It had been arranged that Paul would stay with the Bostons for a week. People would expect them to want to be alone, Joel had told her, and Mike was someone he could trust to watch over Paul properly. The little boy seemed quite cheerful and happy to go with Jennifer and Mike, and watching the guests prepare an exodus towards their cars, Amber felt a distinct sinking sensation in the pit of her stomach.

They left on a drift of laughter and confetti, Joel's arm holding her firmly against his side as they made a dash for the car, but although her lips widened in the expected smile, there was no joy in Amber's heart; only a strangely inexplicable pain.

It took less than half an hour for them to drive back to the house, curiously silent without Paul.

The phone was ringing in the study as they walked in, and Joel left her to go and answer it. Alone in the drawing room Amber wandered about keyed up with nervous energy, touching the flowers decorating the inlaid marquetry table in front of the silk damask settee. For the next six months this lovely old house was to be her home, and yet despite the elegance of the drawing room with its pale cream carpet and pastel furnishing she felt it was cold and unwelcoming. Teri had furnished it, as she had furnished every room in the house, with flair and expertise. Perhaps that way why it felt so alien to her, Amber reflected; *she* was not Teri.

Mrs Downs had told her that after Teri left Joel had had the large master bedroom completely refurnished and redecorated. 'Not that they shared it for very long,' she had told Amber frankly. 'When Joel came home from abroad he used to sleep alone in one of the guest rooms.'

Amber had changed the subject, somehow reluctant to encourage Mrs Downs to gossip about Joel's ex-wife, even though she was curious about her—curious and in some strange way almost envious, although why that should be she found it impossible to tell.

'Amber?'

She came to with a start, freezing as she heard Joel call her name. He walked into the drawing room, lithe and intensely masculine in the narrow trousers that clung to his hips, and the thin silk shirt, betraying the breadth of his shoulders and chest, and the dark sprinkling of hair beneath the fine fabric.

'Sorry about that,' he apologised. 'A business call from someone who didn't know that today was our wedding day. Hungry?'

Amber kept her back to him, staring out of the window watching the dying sun turning the waters of the lake burnt umber, her throat closing suddenly as the full meanings of the words 'our wedding day' burst upon her like a two-edged sword, carrying the total implication of what they should have meant and what in fact they did mean.

The sudden weight of Joel's hands on her shoulders had her stiffening tensely.

'Relax,' he murmured against her hair. 'there are two ways of getting through the next six months, you know. One is with both of us making it hard for each other, with a lot of hassle every time we're alone. The other is for us to agree to put our differences behind us. We've struck a bargain—me because I'm determined to keep my son, you because I was prepared to pay you. Shall we make another? To get through these next six months as easily as we can with respect on both sides?'

He turned her to face him, and for a moment Amber felt the strangest sensation; a dreadful aching pain coupled with a wild longing to fling herself bodily into Joel's arms.

'Well?'

The cool question brought her back to reality, her husky, 'I agree,' drawing an approving smile from Joel's firmly chiselled lips.

'Come on, let's drink to that. Mrs Downs has left us some supper in the kitchen, and some kind soul put a couple of bottles of champagne in the car.'

The supper Mrs Downs had left them consisted of tender fresh salmon and a delicious salad which they washed down with the champagne.

Afterwards Amber enjoyed a feather-light lemon mousse, while Joel completed his meal with a wedge of Stilton. To her surprise Joel insisted on helping her with the washing up while they waited for the coffee to percolate, and half an hour later, sitting in the study, listening to the music drifting softly over them from Joel's hi-fi, her coffee cup in her hand, Amber knew a contentment she hadn't experienced since her accident.

Her mood was broken abruptly when Joel stood up and glanced at his watch.

'Time we called it a day, I think.' He leaned forward to remove Amber's cup, his fingers brushing her lightly. The brief, accidental touch of his flesh against her sent sudden shivers of tension through her. It was ridiculous to feel like this, she reminded herself. Joel had always promised that their marriage was a business arrangement only; he had evinced not the slightest interest in her physically; she knew she had absolutely nothing to fear.

But that didn't stop her from cravenly longing to suggest that for tonight at least she slept in the guest room she had been using since her arrival at the house. Almost as though he read her mind, Joel smiled grimly and mocked, 'Start as you mean to go on, isn't that always the best way? If it helps, pretend I'm one of those men who used to provide you with pretty clothes and expensive holidays before your accident.'

Amber closed her lips firmly together against the desire to demand by what right he took it upon himself to speak so contemptuously—and incorrectly—about her past life.

Perhaps because she was tired, or perhaps because she was nervous, she didn't know which, her damaged leg trembled weakly when she stood up and tried to put her full weight on it, and the sudden blenching of her face drew Joel's attention to her, bringing a frown to his face.

'What's the matter? Too much champagne?' he mocked.

Amber's heart quailed at the thought of the long flight of stairs up to the master bedroom which was at the far end of the upstairs landing, but refusing to let Joel continue to mock her, she forced herself to walk steadily towards the door; the short journey making heavy inroads into her small store of energy and ability to hold pain at bay.

She thought she had been successful in concealing her pain from Joel until he reached the door before her, his eyes savagely dark as he swept her up against him as easily as though she weighed no more than Paul.

'For God's sake,' he protested angrily, 'there's no need to play the martyr for me. Why on earth didn't you tell me you were in pain?'

Without further ado he kicked open the door, carrying her lithely up the stairs and not stopping until he had reached the bedroom they were to share for as long as Amber remained his wife—as long as it took to convince Teri that he would never give up the child she had given him.

Once there he pushed the door shut with his shoulder and placed Amber gently on the bed, before switching on a softly glowing bedside lamp and grasping her chin firmly to force her drawn features round into the light.

'I've got some work to do,' he told her briefly. 'Try and go to sleep. Have you something you can take for the pain?'

Nearly as astounded by his apparent concern as she was by his unexpected consideration in leaving her alone to prepare for bed, Amber nodded her head.

'In my bag. I left it downstairs.'

'Don't move, I'll get it for you.'

He was back within minutes, dropping her handbag on the bed while he walked swiftly across the slate blue carpet into the adjoining bathroom, to return with a glass of water.

Amber reached for her bag, wincing with the sudden pain lancing through her leg.

'Here, let me.' Her bag was open before she could protest, but in extracting the small phial of painkillers Joel accidentally dislodged Rob's last letter to her. Amber felt him stiffen and saw that the letter was open on the last few lines; lines which she knew off by heart without having to re-read them. 'And so, my dear,' Rob had written, 'for both our sakes I think it best that we call it a day. I can never give you what you want.'

He had meant that he could never give her his love, Amber knew, the letter was a reaffirmation of all that he had said at the hospital, and she couldn't understand why Joel's lips twisted so bitterly, until he said sardonically, 'What happened? Couldn't he afford you? You must have been . . .'

'What?' she said bitterly. 'Quite attractive before I was permanently disfigured?'

Joel's mouth tightened. 'You're obsessed with physical appearance, Amber—a fault of your breed of woman; they never seem to realise that there are more important things than looks and constantly wonder why women they consider less attractive than themselves attract men. Is that what happened to you? Did you lose him,' he glanced down at the letter, 'to someone else?'

'Looks are important,' Amber argued fiercely. 'The icing on the cake.'

'Icing can sometimes be used to hide very dull sponge,' Joel replied drily, watching her take her painkillers and then handing her the glass of water. 'Poor Amber,' he mocked, 'did losing him hurt very much? Perhaps there's hope for you after all, then, if you're still capable of feeling.'

He turned towards the door, leaving Amber to mutter rebelliously under her breath, 'What the hell do you know about it?' to his departing and apparently unconcerned back.

Half an hour later, bathed and in bed, Amber tried to relax, and finding it impossible lay staring into the darkness, alert for the first sound of Joel's approach.

It was over an hour before he came, moving quietly and carefully about the room. Amber saw him go into the bathroom, and heard the sound of the shower. Had he known she was awake?

When he returned she closed her eyes instinctively, feeling the bed depress as he slid in beside her, stifling a half hysterical laugh as she remembered how calmly he had talked about this aspect of their business arrangement. It would be necessary, he had told her coolly; they would have to create the image of a happily newly married couple, with all that that implied, but she had nothing to fear.

She had turned on her side away from him, and she could feel the warmth of his body spreading over her spine and thighs even though he wasn't touching her. Almost within minutes of him joining her in the bed Amber heard the slow steady breathing which signalled that he was asleep. An alien emotion began somewhere deep inside her, followed by a sudden, jolting disbelief which totally obliterated the earlier sensation. Had she actually experienced it, or was it merely imagination? Imagination for sure, she reassured herself. Why on earth should she feel *disappointed* that Joel had kept his promise and scrupulously left her alone?

The first thing she heard when she woke up was the birds, singing outside the window. She opened her eyes, looking fearfully at the other side of the bed. It was empty; only a faint dent in the pillow showing where Joel's dark head had lain. Raising herself up slightly, Amber looked round the room. She hadn't seen it properly in daylight before. It was furnished in shades of grey-blue and cream; a predominantly masculine room, with a comprehensive range of fitted wardrobes and a thick-pile carpet which seemed to emphasise its size.

The bathroom echoed the colour scheme of the bedroom. Amber finished showering, dressed in clean underwear and walked back into the bedroom, idly wondering what she ought to wear. They were supposed to be on honeymoon, after all; perhaps Joel might want to take her out somewhere for lunch. Unlike Rob he seemed to feel no distaste at appearing in public with her, despite her scarred leg, but then, of course, she wasn't really his wife. Rob had been ashamed of her; had hated visiting her and had cringed very obviously every time he caught sight of the scar tissue, for all that he was a doctor.

Perhaps the new separates she had bought would be the right thing to wear; there was a pair of trousers with tapering legs and pleats at the waistband which flattered her too thin body. She was looking in the wardrobe for them when she heard the bedroom door open and froze disbelievingly.

Surely Joel hadn't come back? She had thought

he was being tactful leaving her to get dressed alone in privacy.

'Tea and toast,' she heard him call out cheerfully. 'Come on, make the most of it, I'm not going to make a habit of this!' he pushed the wardrobe door closed, and Amber saw that he was dressed in jeans and a checked cotton shirt, the sleeves rolled up above his elbows, fine dark hairs lying crisply along his forearms, his hair still damp from the shower he must have taken before dressing.

Amber literally cringed as he looked at her, in her haste to conceal the imperfection of her injured leg from him, grabbing the first thing she could find from the wardrobe, which just happened to be the silk negligee he had bought her.

'And just what was that in aid of?' he demanded angrily, when she had knotted her sash with shaking fingers. 'Frightened the sight of your nubile flesh might drive me mad with desire?'

Amber flushed under the scorn underlying the bitter words, and shook her head wordlessly.

'What, then?' Joel demanded harshly. 'Look, I thought we made a bargain last night, but if you're going to try these coy, teasing tricks every time I walk in, we're never going to make it work. I have seen the female form before, you know, and ...'

'Far more attractively designed than mine?' Amber brought out in a voice that shook. 'I wasn't trying to be coy, I ...' she bent her head, and her hair fell forward over her hot cheeks.

'You what?' Joel asked, suddenly gentle, putting down the tray and pushing her lightly on to the bed.

'I didn't want you to see my leg,' she admitted huskily, amazed that she could actually bring herself to tell him the truth. 'It's so badly scarred, you see, I thought . . .'

'What?' he demanded, plainly not understanding. 'that I'd run from the room screaming?' Before she could stop him he reached for her and flipped back the hem of her robe, his fingers encircling her ankle as he turned her damaged leg upwards on the bedspread and studied it dispassionately, while her stomach churned with nausea.

'I think you're coming close to becoming obsessive about these scars,' he pronounced at length, 'and letting your bitterness about them colour your entire attitude to life. So you've got some nasty scars and you aren't as agile as you once were—does that mean the whole world has to pity you?'

'I don't want anyone's pity,' Amber retorted, stung by the unwarranted accusation. 'In fact that's the last thing I want . . .'

'Then stop being so damned preoccupied by a few centimetres of flesh! You've still got your life and all your faculties; there are millions upon millions of people far worse off than you. You're a very attractive woman, as I'm sure you know, but you're also a coward.'

Amber flinched, but Joel ignored the defensive gesture, his voice grim as he continued relentlessly, 'If you weren't you'd put down that chip you're carrying—are you sure the weight of it isn't what's making you limp, Amber? It's fatally easy to get into the habit of feeling sorry for oneself—I know I've been there, and the hardest thing I've ever done is to face up to the fact that life doesn't pull any punches, and how you take them is all down to you—you can either be a loser or a winner.' His hand rested warmly against her leg, covering the damaged muscle, and for a moment it seemed to Amber almost as though the warmth of his flesh were affecting some miraculous healing process restoring strength to the fragile limb.

'Remember,' Joel instructed her softly, 'the world treats you the way you tell it you want to be treated.'

Amber opened her mouth to protest, to tell him that she'd never wanted Rob to reject her, then she closed it again as she remembered her own hesitancy with Rob; her shame of her maimed limb.

CHAPTER FIVE

As the days slipped by into weeks and a new pattern of living was established, much to her own amazement Amber realised that she was no longer as completely obsessed by the determination to make Rob bitterly regret abandoning her as she had been when she first accepted Joel's proposal. In fact whole days at a time went by without her even thinking about them, and by some subtle magic she began to notice that when she did indulge in the daydream which she had clung to so strongly during the early days of Rob's desertion; it was Joel's face she saw admiring her new made-whole-again body, and not Rob's. That was because Joel had become so familiar to her, she rationalised to herself, but mere familiarity did not account for the sudden increase in her pulse rate when she heard his car in the drive, or the sense of completion his presence brought whenever he walked into a room.

Now, when he was away on business as he was at the moment, the house seemed empty; the double bed they shared cold and lonely even though he had stuck rigidly to his word and made no move to touch her. He was always up and dressed long before she woke in the morning and always came to bed after her, and yet still Amber missed the warm bulk of his body next to hers, the fresh, spicy smell of his cologne, and the male presence.

Every afternoon she and Paul went for a walk, wet or fine, and she knew that Paul's limp was much less noticeable. A specialist had come up from London the previous week to examine the small boy, and had pronounced himself well pleased with his progress. Amber had deliberately worn jeans and kept still on the settee for the duration of his visit, determined not to draw attention to her own injury. Paul was progressing so well she didn't want that progress impeded by the knowledge that sometimes people did not get properly better.

A close relationship had developed between them. He called her by her first name, which Amber encouraged. There was no point in inciting him to call her 'Mother' when she knew she was not to be a permanent feature in his life. He had put on weight and seemed less solemn than the boy she had first met. She had been delighted to discover that he had an impish sense of humour, although the resemblance to his father when he did smile was devastating.

He sometimes mentioned his mother and the divorce, and Amber encouraged him without asking too many questions, a little dismayed by his stoic acceptance of the fact that his mother had deserted him.

'I didn't like her much anyway,' he shocked her by saying one afternoon as they walked through the woods by the lake. 'And she didn't like me.'

'Oh, I'm sure you're wrong,' Amber demurred. 'It's just that different people have different ways of showing their love.'

'Is that why you and Daddy aren't always

kissing?' Paul stunned her by asking. 'On television when people have just got married they're always hugging and kissing.'

'Television is different,' Amber told him firmly, glad that Joel wasn't there to overhear and glance at her with those sardonic grey eyes. He had warned her more than once that on occasions she seemed less than loverlike, but she found it hard to naturally adopt the intimacy he suggested—and in some ways resented the fact that he found it so easy. But then he was far more experienced in such things than she; he, after all, had been married; and Teri had not been the first woman in his life, she was sure. Although by no means a flirt, he emanated a subtle sexual magnetism that suggested to her that women had always found him attractive and always would. But then, of course, he was a very attractive man.

She stopped walking and stared blindly ahead of her. Surely she didn't find him attractive? Not knowing how he despised her?

Impossible, she assured herself, and yet there had been that odd feeling the first night of their marriage, when she had lain tense at his side and he had turned his back on her.

'Hello there!'

She swung round suddenly at the sound of the cheerful male voice, and found herself almost face to face with a pleasant-looking young man somewhere in his mid-twenties, his eyes so frankly appreciative as he skimmed the fragile contours of her face, and the dark gold tangle of her hair, that she couldn't help returning his smile.

Before she could speak, Paul materialised from out of the undergrowth, eyeing the intruder with a suspicion that almost made Amber want to laugh.

'I'm Tom Forbes,' the young man introduced himself. 'Currently investigating this part of the world with a view to bringing forty children up here later in the year. I'm a schoolteacher,' he added with a grin. 'I work in Liverpool, and this year we've managed to raise enough to bring some of the kids away for a break—camping, you know the sort of thing. Now I'm looking for an understanding farmer who'll be willing to let us use his field at a peppercorn rent. My landlady at the village pub suggested a Mr Digby who farms High Tor.'

'High Tor is the across the other side of the lake,' Paul told him warily. 'This side belongs to us.'

'Does it now? Am I to take it that I'm trespassing?'

Tom knelt down, his face on a level with Paul's, his expression serious enough to make the boy's wariness relax a little.

'I expect it will be all right,' Paul told him large-mindedly.

Amber glanced up, grimacing as she felt the first large splashes of raindrops. The month had been a wet and windy one, and she was anxious to make sure that Paul did not catch a cold.

'I think we'd better go,' she told the little boy.

'Do you live far from here?' Tom asked them, and when Amber explained that the house was only half a mile away, but hidden by the trees, he suggested walking back with them as it was on his way.

He chatted as they walked, making a point of including Paul in his conversation. Amber could tell he was used to children, and suspected that he had a rare gift for imparting knowledge, as she watched him draw Paul aside as they reached the main road to point out the cloud formation racing across the sky towards the Lakeland peaks.

'It's those hills that make it rain so much up here,' he explained to Paul, 'because they're so high.'

'High enough to make holes in the clouds, and then it rains,' Paul agreed seriously. Over his head Amber and Tom exchanged a smile. Tom bent down, ruffling Paul's hair, the same admiring glint Amber had noticed before back in his eyes as they rested on her face. Strangely enough she felt no awkwardness or selfconsciousness with him, and made no attempt to hide her limp. She felt completely at ease with him, laughing as he teased both her and Paul as they walked homeward.

'You don't look like brother and sister,' he hinted as they reached the gates.

'We aren't,' Paul informed him scornfully before she could speak. 'Amber is married to my daddy.'

'Lucky Daddy,' Tom remarked softly, delighting in the faint colour tinging Amber's face.

'Would you like to come in and have a cup of tea with us?' Amber invited, conscious of the dropping temperature and the black menacing clouds piling up overhead. Tom was casually dressed in jeans, walking shoes and a thick jumper, which wouldn't provide him with any protection at all if the clouds released their promised burden.

His frank, 'I thought you'd never ask,' made her laugh, and she was still laughing as the three of them walked into the kitchen just as Mrs Downs was removing a tray of scones from the oven, the warm baking smell intoxicatingly mouthwatering as they came in from the fresh air.

'This is Tom,' Paul told the housekeeper importantly. 'He's looking for somewhere to bring his children.'

'All forty of them,' Tom agreed, eyes twinkling.

'Tom is a schoolteacher looking for a site to bring some children to on a camping holiday,' Amber explained. 'It looks as though the heavens are about to open, so, as he was kind enough to escort us home, I thought the least I could do was invite him back to share your scones.'

Half an hour later the four of them were still sitting round the large wooden kitchen table, chatting away.

'Time I wasn't here,' Mrs Downs pronounced, getting up.

'If you're walking in the direction of the village I'll go with you,' Tom offered.

They left together, Tom eventually accepting a lift in Mrs Downs' car, having promised to return the following day to inspect Paul's train set which was up in his bedroom.

The phone rang while Amber was helping Paul to get ready for bed. Instructing him to finish his supper, she went to answer it, and a sudden thrill coursed through her as she recognised Joel's voice on the other end of the line.

He was calling from Brussels where he had gone on business, and he sounded so curt that Amber wasn't tempted to prolong the conversation, until he commented, 'You sound cheerful, what have you been doing? Drinking the sherry?'

'Nothing,' she told him lightly. 'When are you coming home?' She could have bitten her tongue out the moment the words were uttered. What a fool she was! Her face burned, and she was glad of the miles separating them, preventing him from seeing her humiliation.

His malice-spiked, 'I didn't realise you cared,' reinforced her own opinion that it had been a silly thing to say, and as a defensive measure she fell back on a face-saving lie that her interest had been purely domestic; unless she knew when he was coming home she wouldn't be able to make the necessary domestic arrangements.

It was a weak excuse, she knew, and she waited tensely in the silence that followed, not really able to rationalise why it was so important that Joel didn't think her interest had been personal.

'Don't worry,' he drawled at last, 'I won't embarrass you by turning up at the wrong moment, if that's what's worrying you.'

He had rung off before she had the opportunity to answer, but it wasn't until later, when Paul was asleep, that she had the opportunity to consider properly why she had felt it so necessary to deny that her interest in his return was in any way personal. Why had she felt such an upsurge of panic? Could it be because she knew that her interest in Joel's whereabouts was personal? That she actually wanted him to return, for them to be a complete family unit, for him to stop sleeping with his back to her and . . . She pressed her hands to her ears, getting up and pacing the drawing-room hurriedly. Of course not. Why should she?

Why? Because she was falling in love with him!

No! She breathed the words aloud, filled with fresh panic, longing with every part of her mind and body to repudiate the admission. But once admitted the truth would not simply go away.

Several more days passed. Tom became a regular visitor. Paul liked him and he was endlessly patient with the small boy. He was also a keen naturalist and had promised to show Paul a badger's sett he had discovered.

Although they included her in their walks and conversations Amber was experiencing the curious sensation of standing outside herself observing and watching. She learned that Joel had been right; she had been hugging her resentment and bitterness to her, refusing to relinquish the burden of her hatred of Rob. Now, suddenly, Rob no longer mattered; even her leg and its scars were not as important as they had been. Now when she longed to be whole again it was because she wanted Joel to see her as she really could be, and yet all the time her mind acknowledged that Joel was not a man to be impressed simply by a pretty face, but neither would he accept imperfection in any way; whether physical or mental, Amber warned herself. Teri had disillusioned him about her sex; she had never seen a photograph of Teri, but she assumed the other woman to have been extremely beautiful; and Joel must have loved her once—very much, to judge by his present-day cynicism.

How could she had been stupid enough to fall in love with him?

It was a question she could not answer.

Joel rang again, one afternoon when Amber was out with Paul and Tom. When they got back Mrs Downs told her that he had been further delayed. He was been away nearly two weeks, but according to Mrs Downs there was nothing unusual in the length of his absence. The highly technical computer technology his firm supplied sometimes developed teething troubles that could be time-consuming in being sorted out.

Tom's time in the Lake District was coming to an end. On his last day he suggested that Amber allow him to take her out to dinner, as a 'thank you' for her hospitality to him. He was in high spirits, having secured the permission of one of the farmers to camp in one of his low meadow fields during the summer, and Amber was sorry to have to disappoint him.

'Oh, go on, miss—I mean madam,' Mrs Downs protested. 'It will do you good, and I'll stay here with Paul, if you like.'

Reluctantly Amber allowed herself to be persuaded, even Paul insisting that she must go out and have dinner with Tom.

Tom hired a car especially for the occasion and arrived promptly at seven-thirty, wearing a suit for the first time during their brief acquaintance, his fair hair tamed and plastered damply to his skull. He didn't have a tithe of Joel's sensual attraction, but Amber felt a hundred times more at ease in his company. Because she wasn't emotionally involved with him.

Tom had booked a table for them at a local coaching inn which had retained much of its eighteenth-century air along with its dark oak beams and open log fire.

The food was simple but deliciously cooked. Tom insisted on ordering a full bottle of wine just for the two of them, and somehow Amber found herself starting to float away on a relaxed cloud as Tom refilled her glass and she relaxed under the combined mellowing influence of the wine and the warmth of the logs burning in the open grate.

It was just after eleven when they left. The drive back to the house was accomplished in a comfortable silence that made Amber feel like a lazy kitten.

Tom brought the car to a halt outside the front door, his eyes sad as she opened the door.

'I can't help wishing we'd met before you became Paul's stepmother, adorable Amber,' he said softly. 'You're so beautiful, with those huge gold eyes. Still, if wishes were horses ... What would you wish for if you had one wish, Amber?' he asked her.

She paused. What would she wish for? Joel's love! The knowledge shocked her. What had happened to her? For six long lonely months she had yearned feverishly night and day for one thing, and one thing only—to be made whole again, and yet here she was, when confronted with one wish, wanting only Joel.

As though sensing that her thoughts were elsewhere, Tom touched her arm awkwardly.

'I'll always remember you, Amber.' He bent his head and she knew that he was going to kiss her, but she didn't avoid the kiss, keeping numbly still as his lips burned feverishly against hers for a second.

The sudden harsh glare of headlights imprisoned them in their beam, trapping them like terrified rabbits.

Amber wrenched herself free, half turning in her seat in time to see Joel's tall figure unfolding itself from a taxi.

'What's going on?' Tom demanded worriedly.

'Er ... nothing ... It's Joel, my husband,'

Amber explained quickly. 'Please go, Tom.'

He hesitated, frowning. 'You're frightened of him?'

'No, no, of course not,' Amber lied. 'I just don't want there to be any awkwardness. Please just go.'

She slipped out of the car without giving him the opportunity to argue further. His car left the house behind Joel's taxi, and Amber's slight frame was swallowed up by the darkness.

'Joel, it isn't what you think,' she began stumbling over the words in her anxiety to assure him that the scene he had interrupted had been wholly innocent, but he merely laughed harshly and grasped her arm, propelling her into the house.

'Don't bother lying to me, Amber,' he warned her. 'I've been there before—and with an expert. And what about Paul?' he demanded savagely. 'If you can't respect the vows you made to me, at least I thought I could expect you to realise that Paul isn't a child who can simply be left when the whim takes you—he had enough of that with his mother.'

'I didn't "leave" him,' Amber retorted, her own anger fanned by his refusal to listen to her explanations. 'Mrs Downs is with him.'

'Is she now?' Joel stopped suddenly just inside the house, lowering his voice. 'Well, well, quite the little magic worker, aren't you? Mrs Downs thoroughly disapproved of Teri.'

'Perhaps she knows that with me there's nothing to disapprove of,' Amber retorted tartly. 'If you would just listen to me, I'd . . .'

'What?' he demanded. 'Think of some convincing lies? Oh, no, my dear.'

'Mrs Sinclair, is that you?' Mrs Downs looked at Joel in astonishment. 'Mr Sinclair! I thought you weren't coming back until next week. None of us did.'

'So I see,' Joel commented drily.

'And how did your dinner date go?' Mrs Downs asked Amber, plainly unaware of any tension in the atmosphere. 'Enjoy it, did you?'

'Very much, apparently,' Joel replied for her. 'Would you like a lift, Mrs Downs, or . . .'

The hint was taken, and Mrs Downs left in something of a flurry, her kind face worried. As though he sensed the direction of her thoughts, Joel moved towards Amber with a volte-face that caught her off guard, pulling her gently against him, kissing her temple, and out of the corner of her eye Amber saw Mrs Downs' frown lift and could almost see her thinking that she had been mistaken in her earlier impression that Joel was bitterly furious.

'I'll go up,' Amber said shakily when the sound of Mrs Downs' car had finally faded. 'You must be tired . . .'

'Tired? Hell, yes, I'm tired,' Joel grated. 'Tired to death of women like you, Amber—women who take and go on taking, women who don't give a damn about anything apart from their own selfish desire. Well, other people have desires; and other people can be selfish, as it's perhaps time you found out.'

He swept her up as firmly and easily as he had done the first night of their marriage, but this time his heart thudded unevenly under her cheek; the male musky scent of his body filling her sensitised nostrils as he walked determinedly and lithely up the stairs to their room.

Once there he dropped her on the bed, keeping her pinned there with one hand, while his cold eyes surveyed her flushed cheeks and the slim contours of her body in the new dress she had worn to go out to dinner.

Amber held her breath as she felt those same grey eyes probing the soft curves of her breasts beneath the low neckline of her dress.

'What's the matter?' he asked softly. 'Wasn't that why you wore it? So that a man would look at you exactly like that?'

'No!'

'Liar! And I want to do more than merely look, Amber, I want to find out if you feel as enticingly soft to touch as you look.'

'No!' she protested thicky. 'No, Joel, I . . .'

His mouth curled sardonically. 'Still the coward, but you don't escape so easily, Amber.'

As he spoke he bent his head, imprisoning her with his weight, his mouth draining all will to resist from hers as he forced apart the closed softness of her lips, tasting the hidden inner sweetness, making her delirious with mingled pleasure and pain, her whole body on fire with the potency of his touch. His hands moved over her body, pushing aside the thin straps of her dress, lifting her despite her struggled protests, to deftly unzip her dress and lay bare her pale flesh to his burning gaze.

She shuddered then, knowing that he would not relent, shivering as his gaze became absorbed in the curve of her breast, his fingers touching her flesh lightly and exploratively, before suddenly hardening with the desire she could feel beating up within his body, lending a cruel curve to his mouth and a predatory gleam to the eyes surveying the vulnerability of her near-naked body.

Her flimsy bra was removed as deftly as her dress, followed by Joel's suit jacket and shirt, his skin damp with perspiration, the dark springy hair vitally alive beneath the hands she lifted to push him away.

'So shy and virginal,' Joel mocked. 'Falsely so, as we both know. Are you as cold as Teri at heart, Amber? Women like you who enjoy teasing and running are, aren't they? You drive men mad with your teasing games, but that's all it is, isn't it? You don't have the guts to be real live women!'

'Joel, please!' Amber begged him through stiff lips. 'Please don't . . .'

She gasped as his questioning lips explored the tender skin of her throat, nibbling sensuously at her flesh, sending heady spirals of pleasure shuddering through her; her will power distorted by the effect of his proximity and the touch of his hands and mouth on her body. The clean male scent of him enveloped her; all rational thought rapidly became suspended, the probing insistence of his mouth against her throat drawing a low moan from her lips.

All at once an overpowering desire to touch him broke down the barriers of her resistance, and her hands moved tentatively over his skin, his sudden indrawn breath and slight shudder invoking an instant response from her own body.

'I've already told you, Amber,' he warned her roughly as her hands clung feverishly to his shoulders, 'I don't like teases, so don't play games with me.'

She moved her head, intending to tell him that if anything he was the one playing games, but he moved too, and her lips were pressed against the warm column of his throat. His fingers tightened into her arms, the brief unintentional caress sweeping aside all his restraint. He muttered hoarsely under his breath, something Amber couldn't interpret, and then the full weight of his aroused body was against hers, his lips seeking the parted sweetness of her mouth in a kiss that left behind the child she had been for ever, as her senses rioted into response against the dictates of her mind.

She wasn't aware of reaching up to dig her fingers into the smooth muscles of Joel's back, her body arching urgently beneath him, welcoming the heated pressure of his thighs burning through the thin fabric of his pants. When his fingers stroked lingeringly across her breast, she shuddered in mind-destroying pleasure, her soft moan inciting him to bend his head and hungrily explore the firmly rounded flesh with lips that seemed to burn against her skin.

Vaguely Amber was aware of Joel removing the remainder of their clothing; of him caressing the tender curves of her thighs and the soft trembling swell of her stomach, each caress driving her into paroxysms of feverish longing for an even closer communion with the hard masculinity of his body.

An ache began deep in the pit of her stomach and built up to explosion point, her soft frantic moans soothed by the jagged harshness of Joel's breathing and the increasing urgency with which his hands moved over her body.

And then when she felt she could stand it no

more she felt his full weight slide urgently between her thighs, his mouth on hers as he took her through the barriers of innocence to a place where pleasure mingled with pain, and her heart ached because although he desired her, it was not love, and his possession of her body was merely the appeasement of desire coupled with a bitter wish to punish.

She heard his hoarse exclamation of surprise from a distance; his eyes darkened as he withdrew from her, leaving her without even the comfort of his arms around her.

'My God,' she heard him mutter distantly, 'what have I done?'

CHAPTER SIX

AMBER didn't know where Joel had spent the night. He had left her after saying abruptly that they would talk in the morning, and she had lain awake long after he had gone, filled with shame and humiliation. What must he have thought of her? She shuddered as she relived her wanton behaviour, her complete abandonment to Joel and the ecstasy of his lovemaking. Had he guessed how she felt about him?

That fear preyed on her mind as she showered and dressed in a blue skirt with a matching voile blouse. In front of the mirror she brushed her hair automatically, unaware of the attractive picture she made in her new clothes, her hair curling softly on to her shoulders. Her lips were still swollen from Joel's kisses, her skin a little paler than usual.

She glanced at her watch, dismayed to see that she had overslept. Who had got Paul up?

She went to his room before going downstairs, but it was empty, and yet the house seemed strangely quiet. For one moment she thought Joel must have gone out with Paul, leaving her alone, but as she hurried downstairs the study door opened and Joel walked out and glanced up at her, his face grim.

Was it her imagination, or did he too look a little paler than usual this morning?

'I made us some coffee, it's in the study. Would you like something to eat?'

Food was the last thing she wanted, and Amber shook her head as she negotiated the last of the stairs, momentarily on the same level as Joel and able to look straight into inscrutable grey eyes, before her downward path brought her once more only to his shoulder.

He pushed open the study door and stepped back to allow her to precede him, his thin cotton shirt sleeves rolled up to his elbows, the muscles in his forearms flexing as he moved. Amber swallowed, suddenly intensely aware of him, and the total maleness of the lean body beneath the thin shirt and close-fitting jeans; a body which had last night taught her own to respond to it with careless disregard for the consequences.

'Milk?'

The sound of Joel's voice made her jump. she hadn't realised that he was pouring her coffee, and she blushed as guiltily as a teenager caught out in rapt contemplation of a poster of her idol, as he glanced up interrogatively. She had been too busy studying the lean planes of his face, and the thick darkness of his hair, to notice the deft movements of his hands, and she found herself swallowing again as he indicated a comfortable wing chair, and suggested that she sit down.

Spring sunshine streamed in through the window, highlighting the intricate pattern on the exquisite Persian rug, dancing on the leather-topped desk before touching golden fingers to Joel's skin, revealing its masculine texture to her avid eyes.

'Where's Paul?' she asked him, suddenly remembering the little boy.

'I asked Mrs Downs to take him shopping with

her. I wanted to talk to you alone, and having talked to Paul I gather I owe you more than one apology—not that in these circumstances a mere apology would seem to suffice. I won't ask why you didn't tell me that you ... that you'd never known a man intimately,' he continued smoothly. 'To do so would perhaps be naïve—I can recognise fear, even if I can't recognise innocence,' he told her grimly. 'I suppose you thought I'd come to my senses in time. Perhaps I would have done, if you hadn't ...'

Amber's heart thudded painfully. What was he going to say? If she hadn't fallen in love with him? She tried to speak, but the words refused to come, and Joel, who was far more in control of the situation than she could ever hope to be, concluded, 'The trouble is, you've got such a damnably sexy body; so perfectly attuned to mine that ...' he broke off and touched her pale cheek gently. 'It happens like that sometimes. One moment I was as angry as hell with you, telling myself you were Teri all over again; the next I couldn't keep my hands off you, and by the time I realised how innocent you were, I was way, way beyond any hope of stopping.'

Ridiculously the wry admission made her heart sing, although she fought hard to quell her rising tide of pleasure. After all, Joel must be no stranger to desire; hers couldn't be the first female form he had described as 'sexy'.

'What I have to know is, why?' he pressed softly, coming to stand beside her chair, suddenly dropping down beside her, taking her small hands in his and turning them palm upwards. 'What I'm trying to ask you is, were you waiting for a very

special reason—which means a very special man—
or was that just the way it was through
circumstances?'

The truth was a mixture of both, Amber
admitted. Rob ought to have been her very special
man, but somehow it had never happened between
them, and now she was fiercely glad. For a
moment she was tempted to tell Joel that she had
found her very special man in him, but to do so
would be to burden him with a love he could
scarcely want, and so, trying to be as composed as
he was, she said slowly,

'It just happened that way. There was someone
before my accident—a doctor, as it happens. We
were going to get engaged, but when he saw how
badly scarred I was he . . .'

'Left you flat?' Joel demanded with savage
disbelief. 'My God, when I think of all the
accusations I've made against you! That's why you
were so bitter—because he let you down?'

Amber dropped her head, her husky 'Yes'
almost lost as he leaned forward, pulling her head
against his chest, his arms warm and comforting as
he rocked her gently for a few minutes before
releasing her.

'Poor Amber! My sex hasn't given you much
reason to trust or respect it, has it? Do you still
love him?'

She wanted to say 'No', but an inner caution
warned her that to do so might be dangerous. He
was no fool, far from it, and if she admitted that
she did not care two hoots about Rob any more,
he might realise why.

'What I don't understand is why you suddenly
decided to accept my offer of a job when I

mentioned the money,' Joel continued. 'From what I know about you now that seems totally out of character.'

Amber shrugged, trying to appear lighthearted. 'A girl has to think of her old age,' she quipped. 'I was out of a job; the school had just turned me down, and your offer seemed almost like a gift from the gods, and then once I'd met Paul . . .'

'Ah yes, Paul,' Joel murmured. 'I must admit when I realised that you'd suffered injuries similar to his I thought it really was my lucky day—one moment there I was, wondering how on earth I was going to prevent Teri from trying to take him from me, the next—*voilà*, a readymade wife, who was bound to appeal to Paul. Which reminds me. He and I had a long talk this morning and it seems I owe you yet another apology. He's told me all about Tom, and how he and Mrs Downs persuaded you to have dinner with him.'

'It's all right,' Amber assured him. 'I can understand how it must have seemed arriving like that and finding . . .'

'You wrapped in his arms.' He rubbed the back of his neck tiredly, suddenly vulnerable, and Amber realised how much Teri's infidelity must have hurt him. 'Yes, I leapt to the wrong conclusion—Paul told me you didn't even want to go out to dinner with him.'

'Not really, but he'd been so good to Paul, and I didn't want to hurt him. That's why I let him kiss me.' Her voice faltered, and Joel said savagely,

'Well, now you know just how dangerous compassion can be in a man-to-woman situation. God, it was bad enough when I thought you were simply too terrified to stop me; now I have to endure the fact that you were sorry for me as well.'

Amber longed to tell him that it hadn't been like that; that the way she felt about him bore no comparison to the weak pity she had felt for Tom, but he was too angry to listen, and anyway she dared not tell him. He didn't love her, and for the sake of her own pride it would be wiser to let him believe his earlier accusations were true.

'I couldn't have been more wrong about you, could I?' he demanded. 'You couldn't be more different from Teri.' He got up and went to stand in front of the window. The sun struck right through his thin shirt, outlining the taut masculinity of his body, and Amber felt her heart lurch anew. Dear God, how she wanted him! The longing to go to him and touch him was almost a physical pain. From being a girl of almost cool emotional tenor, she had suddenly discovered fires burning within herself that threatened a conflagration fierce enough to destroy her completely unless she discovered a means of keeping them in check.

'I can't tell you how sorry I am about last night,' Amber heard Joel say. 'Anger is a powerful aphrodisiac; especially when it's harnessed to desire and abstinence.'

The words which he meant as explanations fell like blows on Amber's aching heart. Of course he didn't love her! Ridiculous to think that he might; and not knowing of her love for him it was obvious that he would be appalled by what had happened.

'I don't know which is the worst,' he added, 'breaking my word, or discovering that I'm not as capable of controlling my more base urges as I thought, but one thing I will promise you, Amber.

It won't happen again. Now that I know the truth, I'll make sure of that—God help me, I'll have to,' Amber thought she heard him mutter hoarsely as he turned back to the window, but the words were too indistinct for her to be sure.

'It does take two,' she reminded him bravely, knowing that there had been a moment when she could have stopped him, with the truth.

'Does it?' He regarded her sardonically. 'I don't remember much participation on your part. Did I hurt you?'

A wave of colour suffused her face. 'No . . . that is . . . Not . . . much . . .' she stammered at last. 'I suppose it had to be a little painful . . . and it would have happened some time . . .'

'But with a man you loved, whom you had chosen to give the gift of your innocence, trusting him to teach you the pleasure which would obliterate the pain.'

'It's over,' Amber reminded him. 'And I would much rather we forgot all about it.'

'How very deflating you can be at times, for all that you're little more than a child,' Joel drawled, appraising her flushed cheeks and steady eyes. 'Has no one ever told you that no man enjoys the suggestion that his lovemaking is "forgotten"?'

'But we weren't "making love",' Amber reminded him, proud of the steadiness. 'As you said, you were angry with me; you wanted to punish me, and things got out of hand.'

For a moment he seemed to be looking at her with peculiar intensity and seemed about to speak, but then they heard Mrs Downs and Paul returning and the moment was lost.

'It won't happen again, I promise you that,' Joel

said tersely. 'But I need your help too much to do the decent thing and suggest that we end our "arrangement" here and now. I'm not letting Teri have Paul. She's come close to destroying him once, she isn't going to get a second opportunity.'

It was dangerous to feel so glad, especially when she knew that there was no future for them. Today Joel had seemed more human and approachable that at any other time during their acquaintance; and yet, conversely, never had he seemed more distant. He had taken her in anger and desire, fuelled more by Teri than her, Amber suspected, and she couldn't help wondering just what it would be like to be possessed by him in love. That was something she was never likely to discover, she reminded herself, as the door burst open and Paul came rushing in, cheeks flushed, hair tousled, his limp markedly less noticeable than it had been when she first saw him.

'I've bought you a present,' he told Amber, flinging himself into her arms. 'Look!'

Her present was a rather squashed bar of chocolate Amber recalled having agreed that she quite liked when it was advertised on television, and she thanked Paul gravely, suggesting that they share it after lunch.

'I was hoping you would say that,' he told her ingenuously, adding almost absently, 'Teri didn't like chocolate. She said it made you fat, but you aren't fat, Amber.'

Mrs Downs called from the kitchen that she had poured him a glass of milk and he ran out before Amber could comment.

'Does he often mention his mother to you?' Joel wanted to know.

'Occasionally—more recently.'

'You've really brought him out of his shell. For weeks after the accident we had difficulty getting him to admit that Teri even existed, never mind talking about her.'

'Has Paul always called his mother by her christian name?' Amber asked awkwardly.

'Teri didn't like being referred to as "Mummy". She said it made her feel drearily domesticated. To discourage Paul from using it she refused to answer him when he did.'

Amber's face was too expressive for her to be able to conceal her feelings.

'Exactly,' Joel said drily. 'Perhaps now you can understand why I don't think she should have custody of him.'

'Why does she want to?' Amber burst out, appalled by the impertinence of the question, but it was too late to recall it.

'Why?' Joel looked at her consideringly for several minutes. 'Hasn't last night taught you anything?' he asked at length. 'Emotional relationships between consenting adults are sometimes of necessity extremely convoluted, often to the extent that it's impossible to really define the whys and wherefores, but in Teri's case ...' He frowned suddenly. 'Like I said earlier, she doesn't like to lose.'

Was it that, Amber asked herself, or was it that Teri regretted losing Joel and this was her way to getting him back? With feminine insight she knew that Joel would be a hard act for any other man to follow. Joel had remarked angrily the previous evening that women like Teri were cold teases; did that mean that they hadn't been happy together even before Teri started having affairs with other men? She found it hard to believe that any woman couldn't be happy with Joel, or fail to respond to the sheer male magnetism of him.

The contracts Joel had brought back from abroad meant that he was able to work from home for several days, Amber found herself humming under her breath when she went downstairs in the morning, the day brighter for the knowledge that Joel was sharing the same roof.

He had kept his promise about not touching her again. Amber refused to admit even to herself that she might be disappointed. Her body felt different somehow, more alive and aware, her flesh reacting treacherously merely to Joel's presence. A look from him, however casual, sent tiny pulsing currents flaming through her body. One morning at breakfast he had reached across her for the paper Paul had brought from the front door, his arms brushing briefly across her breasts, and the sensation had remained with her all day, keeping her awake long into the night while Joel slept unaware at her side.

Her obsession with her limp had started to recede; she still wanted to be whole again, but not with the same intense desperation she had felt before. Joel had desired her—no matter for what reason—and his desire had made her whole again in a way that no surgery ever could. He might not love her, but however briefly, she had appeared to be a desirable woman to him, and that thought warmed her even though she knew that ultimately their lives must run apart.

With her hatred of her limp lessening she was able to wear her new clothes with some of her old panache; her landlady had forwarded her clothes, and she had started using make-up again, something she hadn't bothered with after Rob left her. Her new enjoyment of life showed in the happy sparkle in her eyes and the new confidence to her step. Mrs Downs remarked with twinkling eyes that marriage obviously agreed with her, and so when Joel mentioned one day that they ought to think about doing some entertaining Amber felt confident enough to agree. Her mother was an excellent cook and had taught Amber well. She found she was actually looking forward to the challenge, almost to the point of forgetting why Joel had originally proposed their marriage, until Paul mentioned one afternoon, while they were out walking, that the man sitting fishing by the lake had been there for the last two days.

'And he won't catch anything,' he told her earnestly. 'He's using the wrong kind of bait. Tom told me.'

His innocent words reminded Amber that Joel had said that Teri wasn't above having them watched, and she felt disturbed enough to mention the man to him when they returned to the house.

'So, it's starting,' he said grimly. 'I'm not surprised. I had a letter from my solicitors this morning informing me that Teri does intend to contest the custody ruling on the grounds that as a single parent I can't afford Paul the secure background provided by herself and her new husband.' He pulled a wry face. 'I've told him to write back telling her that I'm no longer "single".'

'And do you think that will be an end to it?' Amber asked, already guessing what the answer would be.

Joel shook his head, confirming her thoughts. 'I doubt it. This is just the opening salvo. Teri is a woman who firmly believes in the power of money. She has married an extremely wealthy man, *ergo*, she can buy back her son. Not if I can help it!'

Two days later Joel was able to confirm to Amber that the fisherman was in fact a private detective hired by his ex-wife to watch the house and its occupants.

'She wouldn't . . . she wouldn't do anything silly, would she?' Amber ventured to ask him. They were sitting in the study. By mutual consent after dinner in the evening they tended to avoid the drawing room Teri had furnished.

'Silly?' Joel frowned.

'Well . . . you know. The papers seem to be full of stories about child-snatching, and . . .'

'Not even Teri would be foolhardy enough to attempt a thing like that,' Joel assured her. 'For one thing it's a criminal offence, and for another, I'm sure Hal wouldn't let her. He's not the type. Oh, he'd accept Paul readily enough if it was all above board and legal, but snatching him away illegally . . .' He shook his head.

Amber wished she could feel as confident. From what Joel and Paul had said about Teri, Amber felt far from sure that the other woman would let a little thing like the law stop her from doing what she wanted, but it seemed bitchy to say as much to Joel when he was so convinced that his ex-wife would not seek to circumvent the court's ruling. Even so, she made up her mind to keep a close watch over Paul. The incident by the lake had unnerved her, and it made her blood run cold

to realise that if Paul hadn't mentioned the
fisherman she would never have guessed that he
was watching them. If he had wanted to snatch
Paul away what conceivable chance would she
have had of stopping him? They often spent an
hour or more walking—long enough for Paul to be
hurried out of the country before anyone knew he
was missing, especially if she was not able to raise
the alarm.

An unexpected call from Brussels meant that
Joel had to make an unscheduled trip to the
Common Market capital. He shouldn't be away
more than a couple of days, he told Amber, as she
stood with him next to the car. Paul was watching
some birds nesting under the eaves, and Amber
didn't resist when Joel drew her against him with
one arm, and with his free hand captured her chin,
tilting it upwards.

'Just in case our friend is watching,' he
murmured just before his lips touched gently
against the softness of hers.

Amber fought the longing to cling to him and
go on clinging, but no power on earth was great
enough to prevent her lips from parting invitingly
beneath his, and disappointment shafted sharply
through her when after the barest hesitation Joel
lifted his head.

She was about to turn away when his arm
tightened and he kissed her again, her breasts
crushed against the firm warmth of his chest as her
hands slid over his shoulders to fasten behind his
neck brushed by the soft thickness of his hair. The
languorous exploration of her mouth by his left
her dizzy and yearning to prolong the embrace,
her pulses racing feverishly as desire flooded

through her. Beneath her thin silk blouse she could feel the tormented hardening of her nipples, sensitised by the hard pressure of Joel's chest, and she ached with the longing to feel his hands moving over her body.

'What was that for?' she asked shakily when she was released. 'Good measure? Just in case he missed the first one?'

Joel didn't reply. There was a strained expression round his eyes, and Amber felt overwhelmed with remorse. He must be dreadfully worried about Paul, and more especially because he had to leave him.

'Don't worry,' she told him, 'I'll take good care of Paul for you.'

He paused, his hand on the car door, his eyes unfathomable as he said quietly, 'I know you will. What worries me is who will take care of you.'

He was gone before she could comment, the car disappearing swiftly down the drive. She watched until she could see it no longer, aware that Paul was trying to attract her attention.

'Why are you looking so sad?' he demanded, abandoning his observation of the birds momentarily. 'Teri used to like it when Daddy went away.'

'I'm sure she didn't really,' Amber lied automatically. 'What would you like to do this afternoon? Go swimming?'

It had occurred to her that the swimming baths might be safer than the almost deserted woods, and the exercise would help strengthen Paul's weak leg muscles.

Both of them were exhausted by the time they returned to the house; Amber more so than Paul. Her injured leg ached badly, and she was conscious that she hadn't exercised it as much as she might have done. She glanced down at it as she prepared for bed. Was it her imagination, or did the scars really seem less noticeable? Her doctor had told her that they would fade in time, but she had not really believed him. All she had thought about was the look on Rob's face when he first saw them; and so they had remained in her mind as vivid and raw as the day she had first seen them. It was a similar delusion to that suffered by anorexics, Amber reflected, although in their case the delusion didn't merely involve one limb, it extended to their entire body, causing them to believe they were grossly fat when in fact just the opposite was the case. Women were programmed to place a good deal of importance on visual appeal, she decided; something fostered by magazines and advertising, and yet Joel had told her that personality was more important than looks.

Who was she kidding? she asked herself. Joel wasn't attracted to her. And having an operation on her leg wouldn't act like some magical potion suddenly causing him to fall madly in love with her, she acknowledged with a resurgence of the gritty common sense she had possessed before her accident. Neither could Rob have loved her or she him; had they done so neither of them would have reacted as they had. She had ignored reality and blamed her accident for their break-up rather than face the truth, which was simply that their relationship was flawed. But breaking up had hurt; then how much more hurt must Joel have been by the destruction of his marriage?

She moved restlessly under the warm jets of the

shower. She didn't want to think about his marriage to Teri.

Some time during the night she woke up with a raging thirst and the beginnings of a gnawing pain in her leg which warned her that she had overdone things at the baths. By the time she had remembered that her pain-killers were downstairs, she was so wide awake that she didn't think she would be able to get back to sleep. Pulling on the glamorous negligee Joel had bought her, she went downstairs. She found her tablets in her handbag which she had left in the hall. The house felt cold and her teeth started to chatter. A warm milky drink was what she needed, she decided, abandoning the cold hall in favour of the kitchen, which as usual was gleamingly clean and tidy. Mrs Downs kept it so immaculate that at first Amber felt reluctant to dirty a pan, but then common sense reasserted itself, and she found herself a mug and set some milk to boil on the hotplate.

While the milk was heating she searched for the malt drink she knew Mrs Downs kept in the cupboards. It didn't take her long to find it, and after pouring the creamy milk over the powder she quickly washed the pan, making sure that the kitchen was as tidy as it had been when she came down, all the time conscious of growing colder and colder, to the point where her bare feet were almost numb. Trying to hurry, she picked up the mug and turned awkwardly, shock widening her eyes as she heard a sound in the hall. The mug slid from nerveless fingers, and crashed on to the floor, disgorging its contents and splintering into fragments. Amber moved clumsily to avoid being scalded by the boiling milk, and cried out in pain as she trod on a sharp shard of pottery, wincing as she lifted her foot and tried gingerly to inspect the damage.

The kitchen door was thrust open as she was in the act of hobbling towards a chair, and Joel's lean frame filled the aperture, his 'What the devil's going on!' fading as he saw her standing by the chair, clutching the back for support, her face as white as paper.

'Amber!' He was at her side in seconds, his expression grave as he saw the pain and shock mirrored in the golden eyes. 'What happened?'

She was too shocked by her accident to wonder at his unexpected appearance. Her injured leg was throbbing quite badly, and the shock of the wound to her foot had left her feeling weak and sick.

Joel summed up the situation at a glance, and bent to lift her off her feet.

'Just relax,' he told her softly. 'You mustn't put any weight on that foot until we get that splinter out. Put your arms round my neck—that's it. Where the hell does Mrs Downs keep the first aid stuff?'

'There's some upstairs in our bathroom,' Amber told him weakly. 'Oh, and my pills. My leg was aching, that's why I came down . . . I heard you in the hall and thought . . . I thought someone had broken in and that they were going to take Paul.'

Joel paused on the stairs to push her hair away from her face, as he balanced her weight on one bent knee.

'You're letting your imagination run away with you,' he said gently. 'Paul is quite safe, I promise you. You're the one who needs looking after.'

He carried her into the bathroom and made her

sit on a stool with her foot raised, while he removed the splinter with a pair of tweezers and then cleaned the wound with antiseptic. It was bleeding quite profusely, and he secured a pad of cottonwool over the wound, telling Amber to sit absolutely still while he went and made her a fresh drink.

'Oh dear, all that mess in the kitchen! What will Mrs Downs say?'

'Nothing,' he told her. 'I shall clean it up. Just sit tight while I go and make that drink.'

He was gone about ten minutes, during which time Amber became aware of the flimsy frailty of the nightdress and robe she was wearing and how good it had felt to be in his arms.

'Here we are.' She hadn't heard him come back. 'Let's get you into bed,' he suggested. 'You'll be more comfortable there.'

Amber started to struggle with the tiny buttons on her negligee, her breath freezing in her throat as Joel pushed aside her shaking fingers and completed the task for her with an ease that made her sickeningly aware that she was far from being the only woman in his life.

He insisted on carrying her across to the bed, even though she protested that she was perfectly able to walk. As he lifted her, the fine silk of her nightgown was drawn tautly against her breasts and his expression seemed to change for a second before he glanced away, carrying her through into the bedroom and tucking her firmly beneath the bedclothes. He stood over her while she drank her malted milk, proffering the two painkillers she asked for.

'Try and get some sleep,' he advised her gently.

'I managed to get through in Brussels before I expected, but I've still got some paper work to do.'

What was he trying to tell her? That she was perfectly safe from any unwanted advances? If only he knew! A sob was stifled in her throat, as she watched him walking to the door. If only she had the courage to call him back and beg him to take her in his arms and hold her! Just hold her, that was all she wanted. But for how long? a cynical inner voice asked. Wouldn't being in his arms fan those very flames she was trying so hard to quench?

'Joel?'

He paused by the door, turning gravely to watch her, and the words she was longing to utter were silenced. How could she embarrass him and herself?

'Thanks,' she said huskily, not noticing the sudden cynicism in the grey eyes as he drawled coolly,

'Don't mention it; and don't ask by what means you can repay me—I might just tell you.'

He was gone before she could demand an explanation; and then the combination of her painkillers and the milky drink began to have their effect, and drowsiness obliterated everything but the need to let sleep claim her.

CHAPTER SEVEN

SOMETHING heavy was lying across her body, and she felt deliciously warm. She opened her eyes slowly, stiffening with shock as she realised that the 'something' lying across her body was Joel's arm, golden bars of sunlight from the window striping his tanned flesh.

Somehow during the night she must have turned towards him, and he had curved her against the warmth of his body. She moved exploratively and he frowned in his sleep, eyelashes as thick and dark as any girl could wish for flicking as she tried to draw away. The sunlight which striped his arm laid a golden bar across his face, revealing the overnight growth of beard along his jaw. Hesitantly Amber lifted her hand and delicately touched the rough stubble, holding her breath and freezing as she realised how easily her instinctive action could have woken him. The arm he had flung over her invoked a pleasurable intimacy, luring her into dazzling daydreams where she had the right to lie next to him like this by virtue of the love they shared. Her lips were on a level with the tanned column of his throat. Her heart started thudding loudly as she was swept by a longing to touch her mouth to his skin and let her hands discover the male contours of his chest beneath its covering of dark hairs.

Telling herself that she was insane to contemplate anything so dangerous, she willed herself to move away. But as she did so Joel's arm tightened in an involuntary reaction, and her tightly held breath exhaled sharply as she was drawn even closer into his embrace. Her lips parted, lingering longingly against the warm male-scented skin, its taste so intoxicating that they grew bolder in their exploration, coming to a quivering standstill as Joel suddenly stirred and muttered unintelligibly.

Amber tried to withdraw, but it was too late. His eyes opened, darkening as they looked down at her bowed golden head and wary face, sensual awareness suddenly smouldering in their depths as he became aware of the softness of her breasts pressed against his chest.

It was almost as though they were both enchanted by a magician's spell. Neither of them spoke. Joel moved lazily, encircling her with his free arm to bind her to him, his lips at leisure to explore the vulnerable curve of her throat as he rolled on to his back supporting her slender weight, the pressure of his arms making it impossible for her to move even if she had wanted to do so.

His kisses, at first languorous, became tormenting as his lips rested against her skin in brief caresses, returning time and again to her mouth with a feather-light touch that aroused a storm of need that ached through her, making her long for the passion she was too proud to institute. Her breasts, crushed against the muscle of his chest, seemed to swell and harden, a weak yielding sensation assaulting the pit of her stomach, her small, incoherent cry of protest silenced as Joel circled her lips with the tip of his tongue, tracing their delicate outline, sending stomach-churning waves of desire pulsating through her.

Unknown to her her eyes, normally a clear gold, darkened to topaz, mirroring her emotional shock, shadowed with the intensity of what she was feeling. She heard Joel mutter something jerkily under his breath and the next moment she was lying beneath him with his weight pinning her to the bed, his hands holding her face still while his mouth closed over her own in a fierce hunger, igniting something elemental deep within her, and any other kisses she had known paled into insignificance as she yielded herself completely.

Her breasts might have been made exclusively for the possession of his skilled fingers, so complete was their response to his touch, her small, flat stomach quivering with excited pleasure as her nightdress was completely removed, and she was free to experience the silken pliancy of her body against Joel's male hardness.

When at last he dragged his mouth from hers, they were both breathing raggedly, a dull flush colouring Joel's cheekbones, his eyes glittering with desire, as he swept aside the bedclothes to gaze hungrily at her body, before anointing it with kisses that by no stretch of the imagination were those of an experienced man for a naïve girl, and Amber thrilled to the knowledge that his arousal was as great as hers—a fact borne out by the shaken groan dragged from his throat as his hand trembled against her breast and was replaced by the devouring heat of his lips, grazing the pale, creamy flesh, before claiming the erect nipple on a satisfied mutter. His cheek felt hot against her skin, perspiration dampening his flesh where she touched it, his hands leaving her body long enough to guide hers over the smooth male contours of his, to their mutual satisfaction.

The culmination when it came was a sweet agony that carried her to the stars and left her floating among them while Joel possessed her mouth in a kiss of satisfied tenderness.

She would have been content to lie in his arms for the rest of her life, but Joel, it seemed, had different ideas. Amber listened to him showering, blushing slightly when he walked back into the bedroom wearing nothing but the towel draped round his hips. She longed for him to say something, and as the silence stretched from seconds to minutes she began to worry that he was annoyed with her, that he blamed her for what had just happened.

'Joel?' She spoke his name hesitantly, hating the way he turned away, dragging a tense hand through his damp hair.

'Leave it, Amber, will you,' he said tersely. 'We'll talk later—okay? I've got to go in to Kendal.'

He left just as the post van drew up outside. Amber took the mail, her heart thudding as she saw the airmail stamp and then the American stamps. She turned the letter over mechanically, noting the return address in California and the unfamiliar name. A giant hand seemed to have clenched round her heart. Was the letter from Teri?

It seemed a lifetime before Joel returned. He came in while she was giving Paul his tea, and so great was her concern over the letter that it was several seconds before she remembered how they had parted that morning, painful colour washing over her face as she bent assiduously towards Paul, avoiding Joel's eyes as she tried to coax the small boy to eat another slice of bread.

There was the inevitable delay before they could talk when Paul chattered eagerly to his father, insisting that both of them assisted at his bath, and Amber found herself dreading the eventual moment when they would be alone. What was Joel going to say? Despite their mutual passion of the morning—or maybe because of it—she knew that Joel wasn't about to make a declaration of love to her. There had been ample opportunity for that when he held her in his arms, and something seemed to shrivel and die a little inside her as she tried to visualise what had happened from his viewpoint. He was a man first and foremost, and quite obviously an intensely sensual one, but he was also a man of compassion with his own personal moral code; and Amber strongly suspected that what had happened between them this morning had infringed that code. Knowing th t she had been more than half to blame only increased her feeling of dread, and when Joel said expressionlessly,

'Can you spare me half an hour downstairs in the study?' she knew a sinking sensation in the pit of her stomach which no amount of carefully cultivated optimism could banish.

He was waiting for her when she opened the door, a glass in his hand. She had never seen him drinking alone before, and somehow the glass of pale amber liquid seemed to reinforce all her doubts.

On her way downstairs she had suddenly remembered the letter, wondering how on earth she had managed to overlook it before. She had collected it from the kitchen and paused with it in the door, stealing a few brief moments' contemplation of Joel's long straight back, before some sixth sense alerted him to her presence and he pivoted round abruptly, motioning her to one of the chairs.

As she subsided into it still clutching the letter he turned back to the window, frowning.

'Amber, about this morning . . .' He paused, and she held her breath, praying that everything would be all right.

'It should never have happened,' he told her bluntly, 'and if I hadn't been half asleep and in full control of my faculties it wouldn't have done.'

Her face crimsoned as she remembered the kisses she had placed against his skin while he slept.

'It wasn't your fault,' she began miserably, but Joel waved her protests aside.

'It can't go on, Amber,' he told her curtly. 'Take it from me, in the end it will only lead to problems for us both. I thought I could handle the situation.' He raked a hand through his hair and glanced wryly at her. 'I'd forgotten nature's disconcerting way of asserting herself.'

Again colour washed Amber's face, and she bit her lip, thinking he must be referring to the abandoned way she had responded to him.

'What I'm trying to say is that I'm doing the decent thing and releasing you from our arrangement.'

'But what about Paul?' Amber protested, longing to tell him how much she longed to make their arrangement permanent.

'I just don't know. I'll think of something. I can't in all decency keep you here now, Amber. It would be different if you . . .' He broke off to pour himself another drink. If she what? Amber wondered. If she was more sophisticated, more likely to treat the whole thing casually.

'This came today,' she told him, proffering the letter.

He glanced at the handwriting, frowned, and then ripped the envelope open, extracting several sheets of paper and reading them quickly.

'Damn!' he swore explosively when he reached the end.

'What's the matter?'

'Teri's father's had a heart attack—not fatal, fortunately, but her mother has asked me to take Paul over there for a holiday, reminding me that Paul is their grandchild, and they don't see much of him.'

'You'll go?' Amber questioned.

'I don't see how I can refuse.' He frowned again, avoiding her eyes as he stared out across the garden. 'I've no right to ask you this after what happened this morning, Amber, but would you come with me? I have a feeling that Teri's parents will do all they can to persuade me to give up Paul, and while I feel that I can't refuse to visit them, I need you there with me,' he said frankly, 'as blanket protection.'

'Of course I'll come.'

'Somehow I thought you'd say that,' Joel remarked sardonically, turning to examine her flushed face. 'Have you *no* sense of self-preservation? Most girls would have run a mile after this morning. This time I'm not going to give you my word that it won't happen again—I can't. You're a very desirable young woman and I'm only human, heaven help me! God, what a mess!'

It was the first time Amber had seen him defeated, and she was overwhelmed with a longing to go to him and comfort him.

'Perhaps Teri's parents will give us separate rooms,' she suggested. 'After all . . .'

'They won't like the thought of another woman sleeping with their daughter's ex-husband? Don't kid yourself. They're realists. Teri used to take her boy-friends home with her regularly. I remember after we were married they told me how amazed they'd been the first time I went home with her and insisted on booking into the local motel. I hadn't known her long then, but when I did I was amazed, until I realised that for Teri sex was simply a game, and like chess, you won more when you used your brain rather than your emotions.'

There was a wealth of bitterness in the words, and Amber wondered a little about what his marriage must have been.

'Did you love her very much?' she asked timidly, regretting the question the moment it was uttered. It was a crude invasion of his privacy and would have been better left unsaid.

'I certainly desired her very much,' Joel drawled mockingly, watching the colour mount in her cheeks. 'At least at first. Love is for fools,' he told her curtly, 'or little girls like you, who persist in clinging to outdated myths. As you've now discovered, love and sexual desire don't always equate to the same thing; you love the man who walked out on you, but there was desire between us this morning, Amber, you can't deny that.'

'Who says I want to?' she asked in shaky tones, not knowing whether to be sorry or relieved that he believed her to be in love with Rob still.

'Of course you do,' Joel said softly. 'You'd rather believe that desire only comes with love, but I had to teach you different, didn't I? Amber, are you sure you want to go on with this?' he added, seriously. 'I'm offering you one more chance to bring our arrangement to an end, but I warn you, if you refuse this time, you won't get another chance. I'll have you on the plane to California so fast, you won't have time to get your breath. Teri's parents are very attached to Paul, and it's just occurred to me that when they see how fond he is of you, how hc's blossomed out, they might persuade Teri to drop this idea of regaining custody. They aren't doting parents by any stretch of the imagination. In fact they advised me not to marry Teri. They thought she was too immature for marriage, too selfish.'

'I don't want to back out,' Amber told him, adding bravely, avoiding his eyes, 'and anyway, perhaps now we're both aware of the ... situation ... we'll be able to take more effective evasive action.' She said it lightly, all the time her heart rebelling violently against the denial of her desire to be close to him.

In answer Joel walked over to her, placing his hands on her shoulders and, lightly kissing the tip of her nose.

'Thanks,' he said softly. 'I'm no saint, but I promise I'll do my best.'

That night was the second they spent apart. Amber woke up to find herself alone in the double bed, and thought longingly of how it had been the previous day. From now on she would have to put a stringent guard on her emotions.

They flew to New York at the end of the week, spent a few days in the bustling city seeing the sights and then set off on the second leg of their journey to California.

The heat that met them as they left the aircraft made Amber feel quite faint. She was wearing the warm separates she had worn in New York, but here in California they made her feel overdressed and dull.

Everywhere she looked were young and beautiful girls, vibrant and full of life, wearing brief resort-type clothes. Joel seemed oblivious to the frankly assessing looks he drew as they passed through the barrier and into the main arrivals hall of the large airport.

Teri's parents had come to meet them, and Amber felt her courage dwindling away as Joel started to search the thronging crowd for them.

'There they are!' Paul exclaimed, spotting his grandparents before his father, and tugging impatiently on his sleeve. Unlike Amber, Joel seemed to be dressed perfectly suitably for the hot climate, his black jeans and thin shirt entirely in keeping with what other men were wearing.

Teri's mother greeted them first; a slim elegant brunette dressed in beautifully tailored white trousers which drew attention to her still slender body, and a cobalt blue shirt.

'So this is Amber!' She hugged Amber warmly, and then examined her. 'Paul wrote to us about you. He said you were very beautiful.'

'Children see things differently from adults,' Amber murmured, flushing, as she saw herself with Edie Haines' eyes. Of course she was not beautiful; and somehow she sensed that Teri would have been and that her mother was quite naturally comparing Joel's second wife to his first.

'Joel darling!' She turned to embrace her ex-son-in-law, leaving Paul to introduce Amber to his grandfather.

Like his wife he looked fit and bronzed, in spite of his recent heart attack, and like her he was expensively dressed in sports casuals, his white hair immaculately groomed, only the grooves running from nose to chin alongside his mouth betraying the pain he must have endured.

'I'm sorry to hear that you haven't been well,' Amber told him sincerely.

'Yeah, but I was lucky—a warning—this time. And how's my boy?' he asked Paul, grinning at the young boy. 'Gonna take me fishing?'

There was obviously a good rapport between Paul and his grandparents, but Amber could sense tension in the air when the five of them were in the Haines' car, speeding down the freeway in the direction of their house, which was apparently several miles outside the legendary film city of Hollywood.

It came as a slight shock to Amber to realise that Teri's parents must be comparatively well off. When Joel had talked about Teri being avaricious she had assumed this greed stemmed from a childhood deprived of material benefits, but some explanation was forthcoming when Lee Haines told her that until they had inherited some money from a distant relative quite recently, they had lived in much more modest circumstances than they now enjoyed.

'Spend it while you got it, that's my motto now,' he chuckled. 'What do you say, Amber?'

Both Teri's parents had studiously avoided either looking at or mentioning her leg, although she had noticed how quick they had been to praise Paul's progress, and she wondered again if they were comparing her with Teri and wondering what on earth Joel saw in her.

It was pointless inflicting such pain upon herself, she told herself; she wasn't Teri, and she wasn't beautiful, but she was grateful for the tact with which the other woman's parents avoided any direct references to her.

It was good that both they and Joel had felt able to continue with what was obviously a mutually pleasant relationship after the break-up of Teri and Joel's marriage, and Amber admired the trio for doing so, especially when she saw how naturally Paul chattered away to his grandparents; whatever the problems with his mother, it was obvious that the small boy felt no such reservations with her parents.

The house was set in the hills above the coast; set in beautifully manicured lawns and approached by a sweeping gravel drive. The house itself gleamed pristine white in the brilliant sunshine and was built into the hillside on two levels.

'You can just about see the ocean from the bedroom windows,' Edie Haines told her as the car came to a halt. 'That was one of the reasons we bought the house—the views, and its tranquil setting. Teri wanted us to get somewhere closer to Bel Air, but we told her, what do we need with cities at our time of life?'

'You wouldn't believe how peaceful it can be

around here,' Lee Haines chipped in as they got out of the car, and Joel got their cases. 'Why, only the other morning, I was watching the ridge with my glasses and I saw a bald eagle—quite a rarity in these parts.'

'Can I see it, Gramps?' Paul demanded, his eyes wide. 'Tom's been teaching me all about birds and things.'

'Tom?'

'A young man who's been staying at the village,' Joel explained. 'He's a schoolteacher. Have we got everything?' he asked Amber.

The hallway of the house was cool and shaded; blinds were drawn over the windows, the walls painted stark white to offset the richness of the Mexican tiled floor and rugs. Traditional Mexican furniture emphasised the South American atmosphere of the house, which, Edie explained as she led the way upstairs, was a copy only slightly scaled down of a typical Mexican hacienda.

A beautifully polished staircase led upwards to a galleried landing, again covered with an intricately woven rug, this time Navajo, so Edie told her.

'We've only got the four bedrooms,' she added, 'but luckily two of them have their own bathroom, so it isn't too bad. You'll be the first to use our guest room,' she added. 'It's only just been decorated, I hope you like it.'

Amber did, very much. It was a dream in soft peaches and greens with matching cane furniture and a breathtaking view which included, as Edie had promised, the ocean.

'It's lovely,' Amber told her simply. How very kind Teri's mother was, assuring her tactfully like that that Teri and Joel had never shared this bed; this room.

'We don't have time to talk right now,' Edie told her, 'but later perhaps—I hope you won't think I'm being too intrusive if I say that I'd like to get to know you a little better.'

'Of course not,' Amber told her. 'After all, Paul is your grandson . . .'

'Yes.' Edie fingered the beautifully quilted bedspread and added hesitantly, 'Has Joel told you much about Teri?'

'Not a great deal,' Amber replied truthfully. 'I don't think he cares to talk about it very much.'

'No, no one likes reliving unpleasant memories. I never wanted them to marry,' Edie confessed. 'But Teri always was headstrong, wilful.' She smiled wryly. 'I suppose that sounds a dreadful thing for a mother to say about her own daughter, but we realised before she was out of her teens that Teri would never be the daughter we'd dreamed of having. The things she wanted from life were poles apart from what we wanted for her. Lee was very bitter about her for many years. He hoped marriage to Joel would change her, and for a while I must admit I thought it had, especially when Paul was born, but then she came back here for a holiday, and we soon realised that nothing had changed. She almost seemed to hate Paul. In the end I had to telephone Joel behind her back and beg him to come and take her home. And the dreadful thing is I don't think he would have married her if he'd known what she was really like—but then that was always one of her talents; being able to deceive people as to her true nature.

'After their divorce Joel told me that she had insisted to him that we hadn't wanted her and that she'd been forced to leave home when she was sixteen. She did leave home at sixteen, but not because we wanted her to; quite the contrary. What she did was to run away with some man she'd picked up in a bar.'

'I'm so sorry,' Amber said softly, horrified by Edie's revelations.

'So am I,' the other woman said simply. 'I can't tell you how many nights' sleep I've lost asking myself where I went wrong, why she turned out the way she did, but I couldn't find the answer. It seemed somehow that you only had to tell her she couldn't do something, or have something, for her to go all out in the opposite direction. I just hope this marriage to Hal works out. He's a nice enough guy, but he's not Joel, and it seems to me that Teri needs a firm hand to guide her. Still, at least we've got Paul, and he's as different from Teri as chalk from cheese. I'm glad Joel's found you, Amber,' she added as she got up and walked to the door. 'He needs the gentle touch of a woman of compassion to help heal the wounds inflicted by Teri, and I can tell how much you love him.'

'Yes, I do,' Amber admitted, wishing she could confide in this understanding woman, and beg her advice. But of course she simply couldn't burden Edie Haines with any more problems, she already seemed to have more than enough burdens to carry.

'Oh, by the way,' Edie added, frowning a little, 'some friends of ours who live in Bel Air have asked us to a party they're giving, and you're included in the invitation. I thought of refusing— Julie, the wife, was a close friend of Teri's; they're very much two of a kind, and I suspect she'll try and give you a hard time. As I said, I was going to refuse the invitation, and then I realised that Julie, being Julie, would probably take that as a sign that Joel was pining away over Teri or something equally ridiculous, so I accepted. I hope I've done the right thing?'

'Definitely,' Amber replied with a smiling confidence she was far from feeling. She cringed inwardly at the thought of facing an intensely curious and probably hostile barrage of eyes, all assessing her and comparing her to Teri. 'Do you . . . do you have a photograph of Teri anywhere?' she asked hesitantly. 'I . . .'

'I do,' Edie told her. 'It was taken just after Paul was born. It's tucked away somewhere in one of the closets. Just wait there and I'll fetch it for you.'

Joel and Paul were still downstairs with Paul's grandfather. Benita, the Haines' Mexican maid, had made some special biscuits for Paul and the three men had gone into the kitchen to sample them.

'Here it is,' Edie announced, handing a large framed photograph to Amber.

She could hardly bring herself to look at it, knowing instinctively how beautiful Teri would be, and the reality was no disappointment. Her stomach plunged in defeated admission that Teri's flawless face, framed by a cloud of night-dark hair, was one of the most beautiful she had ever seen, even if its expression was slightly marred by the petulant droop of the full lips and the slight hardness mirrored in the dark eyes.

'She's very lovely.'

'Physically, yes,' Edie Haines agreed on a sigh.

'But real beauty is more than just skin-deep, Amber; real beauty is the look in your eyes when they're on Joel. A truly beautiful woman, in my opinion, is beautiful in spirit as well as body.'

'As I don't qualify for the latter I'll just have to hope I do for the former,' Amber said lightly, her eyes going automatically to her leg.

'Forgive me, my dear, I can see it distresses you, but what happened?' Edie Haines asked her, and because she felt curiously drawn to the older woman, Amber explained.

'And the only hope of full recovery lies in another operation?'

'Yes,' Amber agreed, 'and even then there's no guarantee of success. There's only one hospital that I know of that specialises in this treatment, and that's in a place called Fairlea.'

'Fairlea?—but that's only twenty miles away from here!' Edie exclaimed. 'There's a very large hospital there that does specialise in rare complaints; the hospital was endowed by a millionaire whom they managed to cure of a bone marrow deficiency, and he endowed the hospital very generously in gratitude. You must get Joel to make you an appointment.'

Amber's eyes widened in dismay. Joel knew nothing about her hopes and plans with regard to her operation; he still thought she wanted his money so that she could be secure, and she had no wish for him to know the truth, dreading his pity if he ever found out.

'Oh no,' she said quickly. 'I . . . he isn't sure about me having the operation,' she added in a low voice, hating herself for lying. 'He . . .'

'No need to explain to me, my dear,' Edie

Haines replied, patting her hand understandingly, 'Of course Joel doesn't want you to go through any more pain. I know what men are like—why, I remember when I had Teri, Lee said he'd never forgive himself for what I'd had to endure, but women can endure; that's our greatest strength. I badly wanted more children, but somehow it just wasn't meant to be. I've often wondered if it would have helped Teri if she hadn't been an "only". That's what Paul needs too,' she added pointedly, 'a brother or sister . . .'

'You know that Teri wants to take him away from J . . . from us?' Amber amended.

'Yes.' Edie Haines frowned. 'Her father and I have both begged her to drop the idea. Paul is terrified of her, you know. She used to have these terrible fits of rage—frightening enough for another adult because she'd literally scream herself blue in the face, but terrifying for a small child— and somehow his fear only increased her fury. One of my greatest dreads was that somehow she might injure him when she was in a temper. I can't understand why she claims she wants him, unless it's to hurt Joel. Although . . . Hal's parents are very old-fashioned. They were horrified when Hal told them he was marrying her, I do know that. It must be the first time he's ever gone against their wishes. They also have a very strict sense of family, so perhaps Teri hopes to win them round by playing the doting mother role. They must think it odd that Joel has custody, and for all that Hal is a very wealthy young man, it's his father who controls the family fortune. You see how well I know my daughter?' she sighed. 'I know she can only have married Hal for his wealth—for all her beauty she's a very cold woman, Amber. I'll never forget when she came back after running away that first time, I tried to talk to her, to explain that sex wasn't something you exchanged for material benefits; it was a rare and beautiful experience, to be shared only with someone you loved. Teri turned to me, her face a blank mask. She hadn't the faintest idea what I was talking about. "Sex is a weapon," she told me, "and the most powerful one a woman has, and I'm sure as hell going to make sure I use it to full advantage—which means getting me whatever I want."'

Amber felt sickened and sorry; sickened by the emotional desert of the woman Joel had married; and saddened for her mother.

It was amazing how readily she had been accepted into the Haines' family circle, Amber reflected a few days later, lying by the pool while Joel and Paul swam in its azure depths. She felt as though she had known them for years. Several of their neighbours had called by and been introduced, and everywhere she had met with such friendly acceptance that for the first time she really felt she was Joel's wife—a dangerous mistake, as she had realised this morning. She had been in the shower when he came in, and had left her robe in the bedroom. She could hear him moving about in the bedroom, but had felt no hesitation about stepping out of the bathroom wearing only a brief towel, so entirely at home had she become in the role of his wife.

He had raised his eyebrows when he saw her attire, his mouth curling downwards slightly as he looked at her, his, 'What are trying to do to me,

Amber—force me to break my promise yet again?'
having the effect of making her withdraw hurriedly
to the bathroom, where she remained until he had
gone. And yet the terrible thing had been that for
one wild moment she had wanted him to break his
promise, and not merely passively wanted, but
actively, physically, yearned to encourage him.

Even now she could barely look at the lean
length of his body as he pulled himself out of the
water; without molten heat running through her
veins. His brief white trunks only emphasised the
physical perfection of his body, water running
from the tanned, broad shoulders which tapered to
a lean waist and flat stomach. Amber's eyes shifted
and then returned to cling hungrily to his thighs,
muscled and sprinkled with dark hairs, her
stomach heaving as Joel left Paul to his rubber
ring and loped across the patio to drape a wet arm
across her shoulders and kiss her surprised mouth
with a firm unhurriedness which set her blood
pounding and her senses swimming.

It was only as he released her that Amber
realised their embrace had been witnessed by the
trio standing at the other side of the pool. Who
was the woman with Edie and Lee? she wondered.
She was certainly very attractive, in a brittle
polished way.

'Really, darling,' she murmured throatily to Joel
as she picked her way daintily across the patio on
impossibly high-heeled white sandals. 'Aren't you
a little bit past all that? Or was that hungry look
your little wife was giving you the reason?'

'Was she?' Joel queried easily, shielding Amber
with his body as he stepped forward with easy
grace, while she cringed to think how obvious her

desire had been, her muscles tensing in protest at the blonde woman's words.

'Oh, come on, darling,' the other woman drawled. 'You know all there is to know about women, don't pretend to me you don't know when one wants you!' She had tucked her hand through his arm, her polished fingernails resting lightly on the dampness of his chest, her lips pouted as she glanced up at him invitingly.

Sickness washed over Amber on a wave. Who was this woman?

'I'm not a toy on sale in a shop window, Julie,' Joel remarked coolly, removing her hand, and reaching down for Amber, pulling her up from her chair, his arm going round her waist to pull her against him. 'Amber, meet Julie Arnold. Julie, meet my wife.'

'Darling,' Julie complained with a fresh pout, and a dismissing look at Amber, 'how on earth can you expect me to think of anyone apart from Teri as your wife?'

'For someone who's on her third husband I would have thought it quite easy,' Joel retorted, undisturbed by her acid comments. 'How about a run down to the coast?' he suggested to Amber. 'We don't want to intrude on Julie's visit.'

This time her 'darling . . .' was a protesting wail. 'It's you I've come to see, to make sure you're coming to my party at the weekend. Teri and Hal will be there,' she added maliciously, turning to Amber to say, 'Teri has bought the most divine dress. It's our first wedding anniversary and we're throwing a huge party, nearly all of Bel Air will be there, but as I said to Teri when I rang her, it just wouldn't be complete without her.' She frowned suddenly, affecting a concern Amber did not for one moment believe she felt as she added, 'Oh dear, of course, you probably don't have anything to wear, do you? I suppose all you brought with you was casual things. We always laugh over here at the British idea of casual clothes.' As she spoke she glanced from Amber's chain-store bikini to her own elegant silk dress, at once formal and yet casual.

'I'm sure I'll be able to find something,' Amber said sweetly, moving a little closer to Joel. 'Joel is ridiculously generous, aren't you, darling, so really I don't need an excuse to buy a new dress.'

Julie flushed slightly as Amber's barb found its mark. It was obvious that the other woman hadn't expected her to retaliate. However, seconds later Amber almost wished she hadn't bothered, as another malice-coated comment was slipped sweetly from the expertly painted lips of the other woman.

'Well, you'll just have to resign yourself to losing your husband when we dance,' she said unkindly. 'Joel is an expert, and I for one intend to make sure he reserves at least three numbers for me. It must be quite dreadful for you having to sit on the sidelines, dancing is such a very physically romantic pastime too.'

'As Amber well knows,' Joel cut in, giving Amber a look that made her toes curl up in sheer pleasure, and his soft 'don't you, darling?' brought an angry glitter to Julie's hard blue eyes.

'Dreadful woman!' Lee Haines complained when she had gone. 'Always out to make trouble. Don't you pay any mind to her, honey,' he instructed Amber. 'And I'm sure Joel will agree with me that there's no necessity for you to go to the party if you'd rather not.'

'No necessity at all,' Joel agreed with an abruptness that almost physically hurt after his earlier tenderness.

Was he ashamed of her? Amber wondered. Was he worried about the comparisons which would be drawn; by people's amusement when they discovered just how far removed she was from the perfection that was Teri's?

'I think we should go to this party,' she told him later when they were alone, 'if only to convince Teri that you aren't going to give up Paul. When she sees us together it might make her think twice.'

'I hope you're right,' Joel said bitterly, 'otherwise this whole fiasco has been for nothing.'

His words hurt and went on hurting, and nothing she could do could lessen the pain.

CHAPTER EIGHT

IT was Edie who suggested that Amber should pay a visit to the hospital in Fairlea. It could be accomplished quite discreetly, she told Amber. She would suggest to Joel that Paul ought to have a check-up, and she would offer to take him. Amber could accompany them and could talk to the doctors at the same time.

It was a tempting prospect; all the more so because Julie's bitchiness had reawakened all Amber's dissatisfaction with her leg.

'What have you got to lose?' Edie urged her. 'If

you don't you'll probably always regret it. Joel loves you as you are, my dear, in his eyes your disability ceases to exist, but what about in your own?'

With the fifty per cent of her brain that wasn't yielding weakly to temptation Amber was marvelling that she should feel any doubts. Hadn't she spent six months of her life dreaming, yearning for this moment when she would be able to approach the great hospital which could restore her leg to full normality—and yet here she was actually wavering and uncertain. Her leg, once the focus of all her hopes and ambitions, had faded into insignificance when compared with her love for Joel, and her adult realisation that love was something that sprang from the heart and soul and had nothing to do with physical perfection or imperfection.

In the end, however, she agreed; not because she thought doing so would alter in the slightest the way Joel felt about her, but because she had always known that there was a chance that nothing could be done for her and now she felt she must face up to the doctors' pronouncements, whatever they might be.

Joel made no comment when he was informed of their plans. Paul's English doctors were quite happy with his progress, he told Edie, but if it would make her happier to have him checked over by her own he certainly had no objection.

It was arranged that he and Lee would spend the day fishing, and when they disappeared immediately after breakfast in a car packed with fishing tackle Amber felt an absurd desire to run after the car and beg Joel to come back.

It was almost an hour later before they left, Amber and Edie sitting in the front of the latter's car, with Paul comfortably ensconced in the back.

The little boy's skin, like Amber's was beginning to darken slightly, attaining an attractive tan. He was dressed in a tee-shirt and shorts which Edie had bought for him. His limp was now barely noticeable; the injured leg strengthening as he grew, and he was so heartrendingly like his father that Amber ached to take him in her arms.

She herself looked fresh and attractive in the co-ordinating jeans and tee-shirt she had bought for her holiday with Rob. The jeans disguised the thinness of her injured leg, and that she had started to regain the weight she had lost during her months in hospital was evident by the way the thin tee-shirt clung to the curves of her breasts. She had tied back her heavy swathe of hair with a ribbon, and her skin, glowing with health and vitality, was completely free of make-up.

'How about paying a visit to my local beauty parlour with me before the party?' Edie suggested as she manoeuvred the car on to the freeway. 'Nothing too fancy—life is very casual out here, but in such a way that you know hundreds of dollars have been spent in achieving it, if you know what I mean?'

Amber acknowledged that she did. She had noticed it in the girls she had seen, a leggy, fresh beauty combined with a studied carelessness that achieved a healthy, glowing attraction denied to girls living in cooler climates.

'We must get you a new dress as well,' Edie told her. 'Unless you've brought something with you?'

Amber shook her head. She hadn't anticipated

being invited out anywhere, and she had intended to ask Edie about going shopping. Julie's remarks about her leg still rankled, and she had come to a decision about what she intended to wear.

'Right, we'll pay a visit to Bel Air tomorrow. Fairlea is okay, but you don't get the same class of shop as you do in Bel Air.'

Just after an hour after they had left the Haines' home they were drawing up in the car park of the modern Fairlea hospital, and as she joined Paul on the tarmac Amber admitted to nervous butterflies clamouring for release in her stomach.

Schooling her features, determined not to alarm Paul, who must also be feeling nervous, Amber followed Edie into the large foyer, as different from the hospital where she had once worked as it was possible to imagine. Here the nurses were wearing attractive crisp uniforms; taped music filled the reception area; a girl beautiful enough to be a model sat behind the imposing desk, one wall of the reception area made of glass behind which tropical fish swam lazily.

One thing was the same, though; the dedication and experience etched in the features of the doctors and nurses passing through the foyer, barely sparing a glance for the trio waiting anxiously by the desk.

Paul had an appointment with the paediatricians' department which the girl confirmed, before smiling at Amber and telling her that Doctor Randolph was expecting her.

Amber's heart almost missed a beat. Dr Randolph was the specialist whose work had pioneered the new treatment for her condition, and although she had hoped to talk to one of his staff she had never dreamed that she might be seen by the great man himself.

'Go ahead,' Edie smiled at her. 'I'll take Paul up to the children's unit.'

A nurse appeared from nowhere to whisk her discreetly down a gleaming white corridor to a plainly furnished office, which reminded Amber all too unpleasantly of the specialist's room at home and his final prognosis on her hopes of full recovery.

'Well now, Mrs Sinclair,' Dr Randolph asked, 'suppose you tell me about your injury and then I'll examine you.'

Dr Randolph had come as quite a shock. For one thing, he was much younger than she had visualised; somewhere in his mid-thirties, with a shock of springy brown hair and kind brown eyes. He was also far more approachable than she had expected, but even that didn't stop the waves of nausea washing over her as his white coat and the austere room brought back memories she would much rather had remained buried.

'Say,' he said kindly, on her third stammered attempt to explain to him how she had damaged her leg, 'why don't we just take a stroll through the park and you can tell me all about it.'

As he spoke he stood up and shed his white coat, taking her arm and gently urging Amber through the door and back down the corridor.

Outside the sunlight was almost painful in its harshness, and Amber had to reach inside her bag for the protection of her glasses.

'You must take care that you don't burn,' Dr Randolph warned her. 'With that lovely fair skin you can't be too careful.'

The park he had mentioned was on the other side of the road from the hospital, a pleasant open space dotted with trees and benches. As they walked Amber found herself describing her accident, her reaction to the news that she would probably never fully regain the full use of her leg and her consequent determination to come to the United States to see what could be done there.

'Umm, and yet Mrs Haines told me over the phone that it had been difficult persuading you to come in and see me, which suggests that somewhere along the line you had a change of heart. Am I right?'

'Yes,' Amber admitted. She had never felt happy about taking Joel's money, even in the very early days when she had justified her decision to accept his proposition by telling herself that she needed the money and that if she didn't accept someone else would, but she had come to realise that her willingness to fall in with his proposal had sprung not so much from a desire for the twenty-five thousand pounds but from the instinctive attraction towards him she had felt right from that first meeting. The money and the use she intended to put it to had merely provided a convenient cloak for her real and irrational desire to prolong their contact.

'At one time the thought of having my leg restored to what it had once been was all that mattered; it occupied every single thought I had, but then time passed. I married Joel, and suddenly . . .'

'Suddenly you realised that whether or not you had one leg stronger than the other mattered very little,' Dr Randolph supplied for her, suddenly dropping on his knees in front of her, pushing up the leg of her jeans in a purely professional manner to examine the fading scars.

'Mmm, they seem to be healing very well,' he pronounced, examining the muscles with probing fingers, his forehead drawn into a concentrated frown.

Feeling that they were being observed, Amber raised her head, and saw that someone was walking towards them; a tall, slender woman with a cloud of raven black hair, and features which were somehow familiar. Her breath caught in her throat. Teri! Her mouth went dry, the colour left her face. The photograph Edie had shown her didn't do the other woman justice. She was truly lovely.

'Something wrong?'

Dr Randolph stood up, dusting off his trousers, watching her with concern, his fingers encircling her wrist to test her pulse.

'It's nothing,' she assured him. 'I just thought I saw someone I know. I'm fine . . . Oughtn't we to be getting back to the hospital? Edie and Paul might be waiting . . .'

'Okay.'

All the way back Amber was in a fever of impatience. Did Edie know that Teri was in Fairlea? Julie had said that Teri would be at her party, but what was Teri doing in Fairlea? The suspicion that Teri's presence in the town was somehow connected with Paul couldn't be dismissed. Edie could easily have mentioned it to Julie, who in turn could have passed on the information to her friend.

'Hey, slow down!'

She hadn't realised that she was practically running, until she heard the amused complaint.

'Steady on ... you'll tire yourself out in this heat.' As they crossed the road Dr Randolph took Amber's arm protectively. He was a nice man and she felt drawn to him. He would be good with his patients, she thought intuitively, free to admit now that she would never be one of them no matter what his verdict. When her marriage to Joel came to its inevitable end she would refuse the money he had promised her, and if he drew the correct conclusions from her refusal and guessed that she loved him; well, she would rather be remembered as a romantic fool than an avaricious one.

When they reached the hospital Paul and Edie were waiting for them. Amber's relief at seeing the small boy overwhelmed every other emotion. She longed to rush up to him and hug him to her just to prove that he was not merely a figment of her imagination, but she knew to do so would only embarrass him. He reached that age where in public at least he disdained such displays of affection. At bedtime, when she tucked him in and read his story, it was a different matter!

'Well?' Edie asked Dr Randolph eagerly, 'what do you think?'

'It's certainly feasible that we could restore a good deal more muscle tone to the leg,' he pronounced cautiously, 'and of course any scarring could be reduced by plastic surgery. I've certainly dealt with worse cases, but it would be a lengthy and expensive process. Think about it,' he advised Amber, smiling at her, and then dropping down on his haunches to chat to Paul.

Over their heads Edie murmured to Amber that the paediatrician had pronounced that Paul was doing extremely well and that if he continued with his exercises they should find that the injured leg developed as strong a muscle tone as the uninjured one by the time he was a couple of years older.

Amber was thrilled. She had known that Paul had improved tremendously, and she flushed a little with pleasure when Edie told her that the doctor had announced that Paul's improvement was due in no small measure to whoever had kept him at his exercises.

'I told him about the walks and the swimming, and he was full of praise for you,' Edie told Amber.

As they walked out to the car she asked, 'Are you going to tell Joel you want to go ahead with the operation?'

Amber hesitated. 'I don't know,' she lied, knowing full well that she would say nothing to him. 'I think I'd rather consider it for a while first.' She bit her lip and ventured, 'Would you think it dreadful of me if I asked you not to mention my seeing Dr Randolph? The thing is, the operation would be expensive, and I would hate Joel to think . . .'

'That you married him because you saw him as a means of meeting your medical bills?' Edie supplied with a smile. 'My dear, of course I'll keep quiet. You needn't be afraid that the truth will hurt me,' she added quietly, 'I know quite well how avaricious Teri was, and still is, and that Joel felt very bitter about her reckless extravagance. Every man has a blind spot; Joel isn't mean by nature, but I can quite understand that you feel you have to win his trust on that score. Loving someone is easy, but trusting them requires an act of faith, especially when you've already learned not to trust.'

'You're very understanding,' Amber told her, deciding on impulse not to mention seeing Teri in Fairlea. To do so would probably only upset Edie, who had mentioned calmly after Julie's visit that it was typical of Teri to arrive in California without letting her parents know and without making any attempt to visit them.

'Perhaps it's because we're here,' Amber had ventured, thinking that Teri might have refrained from visiting her parents for that reason, but Edie had shaken her head.

'Hardly,' she had told Amber. 'She would revel in exactly that sort of mischief-making, which is why I suspect Julie has invited you to her party. She knows it will cause a certain amount of embarrassment.'

'And as you said,' Amber had replied, 'if we don't go, it looks as though we're frightened of meeting her, or rather that I'm frightened of Joel meeting her,' she had amended.

Edie had reassured her. 'You have nothing to fear,' she had told her. 'Joel realised exactly what Teri was a long time ago—almost as soon as he married her.'

But Amber wondered if that was strictly correct. Joel had loved Teri enough to marry her; she was still the same extremely beautiful and desirable woman who had left him to go off with someone else. Was the love Joel had borne her completely dead?

Dinner that night was an informal family meal,

with Paul chattering away about his visit to the
hospital and Lee Haines almost outdoing him with
his tale of the fish that got away.

'Amber and I are going shopping tomorrow,'
Edie announced when they had finished eating, 'so
you boys will have to entertain yourselves.'

Although Amber and Joel retired to bed
together as they had done ever since they arrived
in California, tonight Joel didn't adopt his normal
practice of opening the french windows and
strolling round the gardens while she prepared for
bed, and Amber could tell that there was
something on his mind.

'Look,' he said abruptly, almost as soon as he
had closed their bedroom door behind him, 'we
don't have to go to this damned party if you'd
rather not.'

There was a peculiar sinking sensation in her
stomach. Was Joel ashamed of her? Frightened of
how she would compare with Teri?

'I thought you wanted to go,' Amber said as
lightly as she could.

Joel grimaced. 'I don't believe I ever used the
word "wanted"—I thought it politic perhaps, but
then I hadn't given enough thought to the strain it
might place on you.'

Or how it might affect *him* seeing Teri again,
Amber wondered. Calling an old love dead with
several thousand miles between the lovers was one
thing, continuing to do so when in the same room
was quite another.

'We'll have to go,' she said quietly. 'You said
yourself it would look as though we had
something to hide, as though we were running
away if we don't, and ... Oh!'

She gasped in surprise as Joel suddenly crossed the small space between them and took her in his arms, his mouth against her hair. 'It's all right,' he told her, 'there's someone outside in the garden watching us.'

He continued to hold her, and Amber remained frozen within the circle of his arms, fear coiling through her stomach like a snake poised to strike.

'Joel, I'm worried about Paul,' she told him. 'Suppose Teri were to try and do something underhand? She's an American citizen, after all, and you're not, and ...'

'If you're thinking she'll try to snatch Paul, forget it,' Joel reassured her, adding more gently, 'Look, don't let your imagination run away with you. I don't know yet why Teri wants Paul, but one thing I am sure of is that her wanting has nothing to do with mother love, and that's normally the emotion behind child-snatching.'

Amber couldn't agree, but she felt too weak to argue with Joel's arms still around her, the warmth of his body touching hers setting off traitorous impulses.

'Whoever was watching us seems to have gone,' he remarked at last. 'I'd better go and close the curtains.' He started to release her, and Amber trembled convulsively.

'Hey, what's all this? You really are frightened, aren't you?'

'I hate the idea of someone spying on us,' Amber told him huskily. 'It's horrible!'

'I know. It's an intrusion of privacy in the worst possible sense. Come on, he's gone now.' his lips touched hers in a comforting kiss such as he might have given a child, but she wasn't a child,

Amber thought wildly, and her body's response to him proved it beyond all doubt. Against her will her lips seemed to cling persuasively to his, parting, so that he would have needed to be a saint to resist their innocent temptation. As the pressure of his mouth increased demandingly Amber's arms crept round his neck, tiny tremors of sensual pleasure flickering across her nerve endings as restraint was swept away and Joel started to kiss her with the hungry intensity of a man at the edge of his self-control. And she did nothing to stop him! Her lips gloried in his fierce possession, her breasts taut with desire as she was crushed painfully against his male flesh, intimately aware of Joel's arousal, her body melting, yielding, against the hard masculine outline.

'No Amber, not again!'

His mouth was torn from hers with a savagery that left her bereft and humiliated, a dark flush tinging Joel's cheekbones as he turned to survey the hurried rise and fall of her breasts and the paleness of her skin beneath the electric light.

'I'm sorry,' he said tautly, pushing irritated fingers through his already dishevelled hair. 'I didn't intend that to happen, but where you're concerned I seem to have a very low arousal threshold. You affect me as though I were a green boy,' he laughed shortly. 'God, if it wasn't so damned ridiculous it would almost be amusing! Teri with all her wiles left me completely cold, whereas you . . .' He swung round, eyes glittering as they probed the softly swollen contours of her mouth. 'Whereas you,' he groaned tormentedly, 'you practically only have to touch me and I'm on fire for you.'

'I'll try to make sure it doesn't happen again,' Amber said huskily, sensing his implied accusation that she had been the one to blame for what had just happened. If she had allowed him to release her after that lightly comforting kiss, she wouldn't now be experiencing the humiliation of being told that although Joel physically desired her, he despised himself for doing so.

'You do that thing,' he agreed wryly, 'and then perhaps we'll both enjoy some peace of mind. Thank God we don't have to continue with this charade much longer. If I'd had any sense I'd have stuck to my decision to bring it to an end back in England. Your boy-friend was a fool,' he added abruptly. And then he told her, 'And so are you, for going on loving him. If he can't realise what he's thrown away, he isn't worthy of your love.'

He was at the door before Amber could correct his misapprehension, and tell him that she had stopped loving Rob almost from the day she met him.

'I need a drink,' he said grimly from the door. 'And if you've any instinct for self-preservation you'll make sure you're asleep before I come back.'

Joel didn't want her love, Amber reminded herself when he had gone. He desired her, by his own admission, but perhaps he would have desired any woman under the same circumstances. He was, after all, an intensely sensual man. How tempted she was to get up and go to him, to beg him to take her in his arms and make her whole again with the magic of his lovemaking, but pride and some inner instinct for self-preservation warned her that ultimately the result of such foolhardy actions could only be humiliation and shame.

'The trouble with shopping here is that you're spoilt for choice,' Edie told Amber as she parked the car and they both emerged into the blazing midday heat of Beverly Hills' most prestigious shopping centre.

They sauntered past Gucci, closed for lunch— one of the few shops that did, Edie told her, because Gucci's claimed that their clientele was such that it didn't need to shop at lunchtime; it was far more likely to be lunching in one of the more exclusive restaurants in the city. Starlets and would-be actors thronged the busy boulevards, jostling shoulders with expensively face-lifted and made-up matrons, with figures so painfully thin that Amber found herself reflecting upon what had happened to the wisdom and dignity of maturity, and the folly of pursuing a youth cult so singlemindedly.

Edie ignored the large stores, although they did stop to drool over the exclusive models in one of Nieman Marcus's windows and took her instead to a small but very attractive boutique down a narrow side-street.

Attractive striped awnings in gold and black shaded the tiny window adorned with only one dress, but Edie didn't give her time to stare and admire.

'Louise is a great designer,' she whispered to Amber as they went in, 'and in my view produces far more flattering clothes than many of the famous names. She won't push you into something you don't want either.'

That this was true became evident as the owner

of the small boutique first studied Amber's slender frame before allowing her to select any of the clothes displayed.

'I would prefer something long,' Amber told her hesitantly, gesturing to her injured leg. 'Something to conceal this.'

'Mmm.' Louise frowned. 'Long dresses are out at the moment, I'm afraid, although I do keep one of two in stock for more formal occasions, but they're really designed for my older clients, and I don't think I have anything to suit you.' She glanced at the rails and then smiled, suddenly snapping her fingers.

'Stay there a minute,' she instructed. 'I've just remembered something. An outfit I designed for one of my clients just before Christmas—it was intended for a fancy dress ball, which she didn't go to in the end, but it's the sort of thing that's right in fashion at the moment.'

She disappeared and returned several minutes later carrying a billowing mass of rich blue silk chiffon sewn with tiny brilliants, so that it reminded Amber of the sky at night, scattered with millions of stars.

Louise shook out the fabric, and Amber's eyes widened as she saw what it was meant to be; a modern-day version of a harem dancer's outfit, complete with sheer trousers and a narrow tubular bodice.

Her eyes must have mirrored her dismay, because before she could protest that she could never carry off such a outrageous outfit Louise said quickly,

'Before you say you don't want it, just try it on. Full trousers are right in fashion now, and there's enough fabric left for me to make you a simple edge-to-edge jacket to go over it if you wish.'

'Yes, try it on,' Edie urged, and so reluctantly Amber disappeared into the changing cubicle carrying the armful of chiffon silk.

It wasn't a faithful reproduction of a harem dancer's outfit, the bodice being joined to the trousers, its narrow shape emphasising the fullness of her breasts and the neatness of her waist, her skin gleaming palely beneath the full sheerness of the trousers as the fabric fell softly into the gathered ankles with the small bells that chimed musically when she walked.

Above the bodice her shoulders rose creamlly pale, and she studied her reflection wide-eyed for several seconds, only half believing the trans-formation she saw.

The filmy fabric masked her leg perfectly, and the trousers were far more up-to-date than any long dress could have been, but did she have the courage and self-confidence to carry off an outfit which even to her inexperienced eyes carried an implicitly sensual message to the beholder?

'Come on out,' Louise ordered. 'Let's see how it looks.'

Any doubts Amber had entertained were banished when she saw first the appreciative surprise and then the admiration in Edie's eyes as she stepped out into the salon.

'Oh, my dear!' she exclaimed a little breathlessly. 'You'll cause a positive riot—won't she, Louise?'

'Most definitely,' the other woman laughed. 'I don't normally go in for such sexy outfits, I've never considered them my forte, but looking at this one, I'm beginning to wonder if I haven't mistaken my vocation. It just needs something to complete it, and I've got the very thing.' She disappeared and then returned carrying a wide silver leather belt higher at the front than at the back, which she placed round Amber's waist and then laced up in the manner Amber had seen in rollicking period films, as worn by buxom country wenches.

When she pulled a face, Louise assured her seriously, 'It's just what it needs to add that gimmicky touch that's all the rage at the moment. Everyone's into this nostalgic dressing up.'

'But it makes me look . . .' Amber stared into the mirror, unable to correctly define the way in which the silver belt emphasised her waist and drew subtle attention to the swell of her breasts.

'It makes you look like a very desirable wanton,' Louise finished frankly for her. 'Which is exactly what it ought to do. There's a pair of silver slippers to go with it—what size are you?' she asked.

As it happend the slippers were exactly Amber's size, pretty curly-toed affairs which added to the Arabian Nights quality of her outfit.

'All you need now is a very sexy hairstyle and a little bit of theatrical make-up,' Louise told her.

'We're going to my beauty parlour before the party,' Edie told her, mentioning a name which was obviously familiar to Louise. 'Ask for Rick,' she told Amber, 'and tell him what you're wearing.'

A little afraid that she would never have the confidence to carry off both the outfit and the type of make-up Louise was suggesting, Amber paid for the outfit, and followed Edie out into the sunshine.

'You don't think it's a little bit . . . well . . .'

'Sexy?' the older women suggested, eyes twinkling. 'More than a little, my dear, but in the nicest possible way. You looked delightful, although I suspect you'd better stick pretty close to Joel, I doubt any man with red blood in his veins will be able to look at you in that outfit without wanting to remove it.' She laughed at Amber's shocked expression, and added wickedly, 'Isn't that what you'll want Joel to do? I can't wait to see Julie's face when she sees you. She'll be green!'

And Teri? Amber wanted to ask. How would she feel? But it was a question she simply couldn't voice.

CHAPTER NINE

THE party was in full swing by the time Joel, Amber and the Haineses reached the Beverly Hills mansion owned by Julie and her film producer husband.

Amber still wasn't sure whether she had done the right thing in wearing the outfit she had bought with Edie, neither did she feel entirely comfortable with the exotic make-up and hair-do fashioned for her by the experts at Edie's beauty salon.

It was true that Joel's expression had changed when he saw her in all her finery, but the look he had given her had been probing and reserved rather than admiring, and she wondered cringingly if she was making a fool of herself by wearing such an exotic outfit and whether it wouldn't have been wiser to wear something less attention-seeking.

'Joel, you haven't told Amber how attractive she looks,' Edie scolded as they left the car. 'And I'm sure if you don't, there'll be plenty of other men in evidence tonight who will.'

Joel's laconic, and almost contemptuous, 'So am I,' left Amber feeling even more vulnerable than before.

Julie detached herself from a crowd in the huge drawing room to welcome them, her arm through Joel's as she drew him forward to introduce him around, Amber lagging selfconsciously behind, aware of curious glances.

Behind the enormous living room was a partially enclosed patio with a stylish swimming pool and gardens beyond illuminated with tiny lights. The guests were mainly in their twenties and thirties, sophisticated, 'wordly creatures among whom Amber felt completely alien.

Ahead of them a small knot of people suddenly parted, an expectant silence falling on the room as the dark-haired woman in the revealing scarlet silk dress stepped forward. There was self-confidence in her sensual walk, in the deliberately erotic movement of her head to reveal the slender lissomness of her throat and the full tautness of breasts barely covered by the revealing scarlet silk, and even if she had not recognised her from her photograph and her brief sighting of her in Fairlea, Amber would have recognised Teri by the way she claimed Joel, the mocking, dismissive look she gave Amber, bringing to mind the words 'to the victor the spoils.' But Joel was a man with a mind of his own who had already told her how he felt about his ex-wife. If he had told her the truth he was an excellent actor, she thought bitterly seconds later, watching the careless insouciance with which he raised the scarlet-tipped fingers to his lips, his eyes slumbrous and smoky as he said softly,

'Dare I hope that you're here alone?'

Pain like an iron band tightened around Amber's heart. She could barely see Teri's triumphant smile for the tears blurring her eyes, but nothing could blot out the triumph in the other woman's voice as she darted a malicious glance at Amber and replied huskily, 'I'm afraid not, darling. Unlike you, Hal isn't quite so careless with his possessions.'

'What a wise man!'

'You haven't introduced me to your new wife yet, darling,' Teri reminded him, having basked sufficiently in his admiration. 'Poor little thing, she looks terribly left out, although of course appearances can be deceptive, can't they?'

As Joel introduced them, she said sweetly to Amber, 'Didn't I see you in Fairlea the other day?'

'Amber was taking Paul to the hospital for his check-up,' Joel told her.

Teri's eyebrows rose in amusement. 'Really? When I saw her she was enjoying a tête-à-tête with a most attractive man in the park. Poor little Paul wasn't anywhere in sight—oh dear!' she added sweetly, looking from Joel's frowning face to Amber's pale one. 'Have I put my foot in it?'

In the gardens a group started playing modern music and once again Teri took possession of Joel's arm, darting Amber a mocking look. 'Come and dance with me, darling,' she pleaded. 'Hal has two left feet, and of course poor little Amber couldn't possibly . . .' She looked down at Amber's leg. 'It must be dreadful for you,' she said carelessly, 'and for Joel, of course.'

With that parting thrust she swept Joel away, leaving Amber wanting to creep away somewhere where no other cruel eyes could witness her vulnerability.

She turned and almost stumbled, shocked upright by the firm clasp of male fingers on her arm. Laughing blue eyes looked down into hers out of a lean, tanned, masculine face.

'Hey, careful there!' a deep baritone cautioned. 'You all right?'

'Fine,' Amber assured her rescuer shakily. 'Thanks for saving me.'

'As a reward, you can let me get you a drink. You're English, aren't you?' he questioned, as he shepherded Amber through the crowd, without giving her an opportunity to refuse. 'Been out here long?'

'Only a few days. And you?'

'Born and bred,' he told her with a grin. 'My folks have always been in the movie business and I kinda just naturally followed suit. You here alone?' he asked, eyeing her slender form appreciatively. 'You're a very attractive girl, but somehow you don't look like the normal anxious-to-make-it starlet.'

Amber laughed, 'I'm flattered that you thought I might be. Actually I'm here with my husband, and invited only as an afterthought. Are you here alone?'

'Yup. Julie is my sister-in-law and invites me to her parties as a kinda makeweight. Say,' he said suddenly, frowning, 'you aren't Joel's wife, are you? No, you can't be.' He shook his head, to himself. 'Julie said she was . . .'

'Crippled?' Amber supplied for him in a tight little voice. 'Oh, please,' she added when she saw his give-away expression, 'don't try to pretend. She gestured to her leg. 'What's the point in hiding the truth? Would you like to see the scars?' she almost threw at him, knowing she was behaving badly but totally unable to do anything about it. Over his shoulder her eyes kept sliding to the gardens, hunting for Joel's familar figure, a tight aching pain centring round her heart.

'Lost someone?' the pleasant voice drawled, as he followed her gaze.

'I'm sorry about what I just said,' Amber apologised. 'It was unforgivable, but . . .'

'But my dear sweet sister-in-law has been sticking the knife in?' He laughed bitterly at Amber's silence. 'Oh, believe me, there's nothing you can tell me about Julie, I know it all. She's a first-class bitch.'

Over his shoulder Amber suddenly saw Joel walking past. Teri was clinging to his arm, her face raised to his. They stopped, oblivious to anyone but themselves. Teri swayed seductively against Joel, and sickness clawed at Amber's stomach as she turned blindly away.

'Hey, come on, it can't be that bad,' her rescuer joked. 'Look, how about exchanging names? I'm Chet, and you?'

Amber mumbled her name.

'Amber,' Chet repeated. 'Suits you. Look,' he said suddenly, 'let me give you a piece of advice. Forget my bitchy sister-in-law and her kind—the world is full of them, and they'll turn it into a hell for you if they can, but always remember that their desire to hurt springs from an inner deep-seated deficiency within themselves. It has to do. Ask yourself one thing, do truly happy people need to score off others?' When Amber shook her head, he grinned. 'Well, just remember that. Come on,' he added, 'you and I are going to dance. You look like a moonbeam in that get-up.'

Chat's presence at her side restored a little of Amber's self-confidence, and following hard on the heels on her bitter despair came a dangerous recklessness telling her that no matter what she did now she had nothing to lose—she had lost it all when Joel walked away with Teri!

Chet was an excellent dancer, light on his feet, their steps matching so perfectly that Amber felt as though she was dancing on air. The tempo of the music changed, to a slow, sensuous beat, the lights dimming as couples moved closer together. Amber was about to suggest that they returned to the house when she caught a glimpse of a familiar male back. Jealousy burned through her, making her as pliable as silk in Chet's arms when they closed about her.

'Are you just an illusion, moonbeam girl?' he murmured against her cheek. 'If I kiss you will you turn into a small heap of stardust at my feet?' His lips moved gently against her skin. Slowly and expertly he was manoeuvring them away from the other dancers into the shadows.

If she kept her eyes tightly closed she could always pretend it was Joel holding her, Amber deceived herself, but they flew open when a hard hand descended on her arm, and steel fingers dug into her flesh as she was wrenched away from Chet.

'Joel!' Her husband's name escaped Amber's lips on a startled gasp.

'Yes, Joel,' he repeated bitterly. 'Did you think I was safely out of the way? Is that why you allowed him to paw you? What did he do—offer you a bit part in his new movie?'

'Now just a minute,' Chet interrupted angrily. 'It wasn't anything like that. We were just dancing . . .'

'But you wouldn't have much longer, would you?' Joel demanded coldly. 'If it wasn't for the fact that I'm pretty sure I know exactly who's to blame, you and I would have a score to settle.' He turned to Amber. 'And as for you . . .'

'Look . . .' Chet began, stepping forward, his hand on Joel's arm.

Joel threw it off, and snarled at Chet, 'Hasn't anyone ever warned you about coming between a man and wife? We're leaving,' he told Amber. 'Now!'

Chet tried to intervene, but Joel thrust him aside bodily, almost dragging Amber behind him. She tried to remind him that they couldn't simply just leave without telling the Haines, but he refused to listen to her.

During the taxi ride back to the house a heavy, threatening silence emanated from him. Amber scarcely recognised him in this dangerous mood. What had brought it on? Seeing Teri again and realising what he had lost?

'Out,' he said curtly when the taxi stopped. She climbed out of the taxi clumsily, leaving Joel to pay the driver, his footsteps behind her starting up dread in the pit of her stomach. There was something alien and implacable about him that set off alarm bells within her.

'I'm tired,' she told him breathlessly once they were inside. 'If you don't mind, I think I'll go to bed.'

She knew she had made a mistake the moment she saw the expression in Joel's eyes.

'Oh, I don't mind at all,' he told her silkily. 'In fact it's exactly what I had in mind. You look extremely desirable in that houri outfit, and I wasn't the only man to think so tonight, was I? Tell me,' he continued in that same hateful voice, 'have you been practising crawling up between the sheets in the approved manner, or was your new friend so hot for you that he wasn't concerned with the preliminaries?'

'He kissed me, that's all,' Amber threw at him, hating his cruel insinuations. 'Just a kiss . . .'

She turned as she spoke, stumbling along the passage to their room. Joel was right behind her, barring her attempt to close the door on him.

'Just a kiss?' he asked smoothly. 'How blasée you've become!' He was reaching for her as he spoke, making it impossible for her to evade his cruel hands, the twisted smile drawing down his mouth making panic explode inside her in terror-stricken waves.

'But it wouldn't have stopped there, would it, Amber? Don't bother to lie! I saw the way he was looking at you—what he was thinking, just as I'm thinking now. But that's the difference between us, Amber. All he could do was look and think, while I . . .'

As he spoke his mouth closed fiercely on hers, its pressure sapping her strength, draining her frail reserves of detachment. Her breath rose in her throat in an aching sob as his fingers left her upper arms to move over her shoulders, grasping the front of her outfit.

'I can do much more than look,' he finished hoarsely, releasing her bruised mouth momentarily.

'Joel,' she pleaded desperately, 'please don't do this . . .'

'You'll have to do better than that,' he mocked. 'I can make you want me, Amber.' And as though to prove his point his hand slid seductively over the curve of her breast, caressing it to aching awareness, her breath tightening in her chest as she tried to escape the inevitable pain.

'Joel, please . . .' she tried again, but his hand only reinforced its arrogant possession of her breast.

'Please what?' he grated. 'Forget what I saw? Forget how willingly you went into his arms, allowed him to touch you, to kiss you? Oh no, Amber,' he said softly, 'you're the one who's going to forget—everything but the feel of my hands against your body, my mouth on yours, my body possessing yours.'

Sickness welled inside her. On the periphery of her awareness she felt Joel's brutal tug on the fine fabric of her outfit, heard the sharp tearing sound, and felt the cool shaft of air against her skin. And then the coolness was replaced by the surging heat of Joel's hands, savagely pushing aside the torn fabric, and possessing the soft fullness of her breasts, not with tenderness, but with a primaeval force that seemed to find an echo in her own body, the anger fear had previously suppressed rising up in a force to match Joel's own.

Whoever it was who had said that anger was a potent aphrodisiac had known what they were talking about, she decided hazily as Joel lifted her, carrying her swiftly to the bed, and laying her upon it, pausing, she realised seconds later when the fierce heat of his flesh covered hers, to remove his own clothes, his mouth clamping down on hers with a message that transcended everything but her body's own urgent response to it.

Later, she told herself she would feel shame for this, but right now all that mattered was her body's urgent response to Joel's touch; the ferocity of the fires he had lit, and which smouldered hungrily everywhere that his hands and lips touched. His tongue traced a sensuous trail along her neck, capturing the frantic pulse beating there, forcing from her aching throat a husky moan of surrender.

Her fingers sought the breadth of his shoulders in protest, the damp heat of his skin beneath her palms erasing her intention to push him aside, substituting in its stead a desire to explore the hard purity of his muscles, tautening as she touched, tiny shock waves of pleasure coursing through her body at the touch of his flesh, male and alien and subtly exciting.

Joel muttered a protest against her mouth as her fingers slid from his chest to the clenched hardness of his stomach, while his own hands swept fiercely over her body, moulding her waist, and then sliding to her hips, appeasing her need for him by lifting her against him, the rasp of his hair-roughened thigh against her own smooth flesh infinitely pleasurable.

Her wayward flesh responding against the dictates of common sense, Amber abandoned her attempts to withstand the combined force of their mutual desire, her small cries of pleasure as Joel's tongue teased her nipples into aroused awareness finding an echo in his own hoarse demand to feel her mouth against his skin.

She complied with lips that trembled slightly as they traced a delicate path across his shoulders, feeling with the sudden tensing of his muscles the effect she was having on him. His fingers tightened in her hair, drawing her down against him, but once tasted his flesh was like a heady drug and her lips moved feverishly over his chest, feeling the urgent thudding of his heart beneath the crisply curling dark hairs, and then lower, thrilling to the convulsive shudders racking his body as her tongue traced a delicate path across his flat stomach, knowing that his arousal matched her own; that he was no longer the cool, urbane stranger she had first known, nor the angry, punishing husband who had brought her to this room, but a man shaking with the desire to possess her.

His hands pulled her upwards and slid to her wrists, pinning her to the bed with masculine dominance. She struggled briefly to be free, her body aching for his.

'How I want you,' Amber heard him mutter hoarsely as he looked down at her. 'The way I feel at the moment, a whole lifetime wouldn't be long enough to appease my desire.' He bent towards her and Amber closed her eyes, her whole body poised and waiting . . .

Seconds ticked by, then her wrists were released. She felt the bed move and opened her eyes. Joel was sitting on the side of it with his back to her.

'It's no good,' he told her brutally. 'Without love it doesn't mean a thing.' He turned and saw her expression before she could mask it and said savagely, 'What's wrong? You ought to be thanking your lucky stars I came to my senses, not looking at me as though...'

'As though I want you to make love to me?' Amber said tightly. 'Women experience desire too, you know,' she told him, desperate to retrieve her pride. 'Love and sex don't always go hand in hand.'

'Don't I just know it?' Joel agreed grimly. 'If it was feasible I'd suggest we had separate rooms, but it isn't. Lee has a bottle of Scotch in his den,' he went on. 'They tell me it's an excellent anaesthetic. You'd better just pray that that's true, because despite all you've said and done I still don't think you're the kind of woman who can find oblivion in sex for sex's sake. Oh, you've tried pretty hard to prove it tonight,' he added bitterly. 'First that guy at the party and now me, but we both know it doesn't work, don't we?'

He was gone before Amber could speak. She watched him go in mute agony, longing to call him back, but prevented by her pride. Later she would probably feel glad, but right now it was pure, undiluted hell.

'You two left the party early,' Edie Haines commented at breakfast, her eyes twinkling. 'Now that's what I call romance! I can't remember the last time we left a party early, Lee, so that we could be alone, can you?'

Amber managed a strained smile, although it was more than she could do to look at Joel. The atmosphere between them was so fraught with tension that she was almost relieved when he announced halfway through the morning that he had to go out. Where to? she wondered jealously when he had gone. To see Teri?

He had been gone about an hour when the telephone rang. Amber and Paul were alone in the house, Julie having telephoned Edie to ask her to go over with Lee as Teri wanted to see them.

'I don't like to leave you alone like this,' Edie apologised, 'but Julie said it was quite urgent, although knowing Teri it will probably be something trivial. It's my guess that she's regretting leaving Joel,' she added without thinking. 'Oh, my dear,' she apologised remorsefully, 'how tactless of me! I didn't mean to imply . . .'

'Oh, it's all right,' Amber assured her, forcing a bright smile. 'To tell you the truth, I got the impression at the party last night that Teri was still very . . . fond of Joel.'

'Oh, she always was possessive. I suspect she can't bear to think that someone else has taken her place. I hope we aren't going to have to endure one of her tantrums.'

Amber let the phone ring, but when the shrill noise persisted, she decided it would be better to answer. To her amazement the voice on the other end of the line asked for her.

'Mrs Sinclair speaking,' she said uncertainly. 'Who is that?'

'It's Fairlea hospital, Mrs Sinclair,' came the reply. 'Dr Burns would like you to come right down here with Paul—something to do with one of the X-rays they took when you visited.'

Dr Burns was the paediatrician, and fear stabbed through her. 'I don't have a car,' she protested. If only Joel was here, or even the Haineses.

'Order a cab, Mrs Sinclair,' the brisk female voice suggested in the tones of someone used to dealing with confused patients. 'Or better still, I'll give you the number of a service we use. They have a depot in your area, please hold a moment and I'll look it up for you.'

The brief seconds she had to wait for the number felt like aeons to Amber, in a fever of impatience to get to the hospital and see Dr Burns. She knew better than to ask to speak to him on the phone. Doctors preferred to talk in person, she knew that from her own experience, especially when it was bad news. 'Stop it!' she warned herself fiercely, quickly jotting down the number the girl gave her. Her fingers trembled as she dialled it. She could hear Paul playing in the living room, and she felt cold with dread. If only Joel were here!

At last someone answered, a laconic male voice promising a car within ten minutes. The phone rang while she was urging Paul into clean jeans and tee-shirt, and as she raced to answer it Amber prayed that it might be Joel. It wasn't; it was Chet.

'I hope I didn't get you into hot water last night?' he asked. 'That's one hell of a jealous husband you have there. And I always thought the British male was unemotional!'

Amber cut him short, explaining that she had to take Paul to the hospital, surprised to see when she replaced the receiver that she had doodled Chet's name on the pad where she had jotted down the taxi firm's number.

She barely had time to find her handbag and check her purse for money before the taxi had arrived and its driver was striding up to the door.

All the way along the freeway Amber's nerves were stretched to breaking point as she tried to keep Paul occupied, striving to appear natural and unconcerned.

'But why do they want to see me?' he demanded for the umpteenth time. 'The doctor told me I was fine.'

'Of course you are,' Amber agreed with a confidence she was far from feeling. 'They just want to do some more tests. Tests that will probably help other children,' she told him, hating herself for lying, but what was the point in both of them panicking? Let Paul enjoy peace of mind for just as long as he could!

After several miles they turned off the freeway, where the road curved upwards towards the hills; a different route from the one she had taken with Edie. It seemed to go on for ever; the countryside around them growing increasingly desolate, almost bordering on desert; patches of scrub interspersed with sandy slopes, a bareness about the landscape that made Amber shiver a little despite the blazing heat of the sunshine. Perhaps it was the car's air-conditioning, she thought, rubbing her goose-fleshed arms, and wondering why it was that the journey seemed to be taking so long. She glanced at her watch and frowned. It was closer to ninety minutes than sixty since they had left the house, and she was reasonably sure that when she went to

Fairlea with Edie it had taken barely an hour.

'Are you sure you know the way?' she demanded of the driver, leaning forward to address him, her voice sharper than usual, as she added tensely, 'You do know where we're going?'

'Sure I do, lady,' came the drawled response. 'And right here is where you get out. That's if you've any sense. From here if you start walking back down that track you should be lucky enough to get a lift before nightfall.'

'You . . . I . . .' Amber stared at him in shocked silence as he suddenly braked and stopped the car on the lonely, dusty road.

'What are you doing?' she demanded wildly as the driver pushed open her door. 'What's going on?'

'You ask too many questions, lady,' she was told in a newly hard voice. 'Just get out, and forget all about this.'

'But Paul . . .' she started to protest, only to be silenced by the man's laconic,

'The kid will be fine with me. I don't aim to hurt him. His ma wouldn't like that.'

CHAPTER TEN

IT was several seconds before the truth filtered through to Amber's numb brain.

'You've kidnapped him,' she said shakily at last. 'On his mother's instructions, so that she can claim custody. But you can't . . . It's illegal . . .'

'Possession is nine tenths of the law,' the man reminded her. 'This isn't the first custody case I've handled and it won't be the last. Now be a good little girl and just run along. No one wants to hurt you.'

No one had obviously told him that she was Paul's stepmother, Amber realised, wondering how she could best turn that omission into an advantage. But first one thing had to be made crystal clear.

'I'm not going anywhere,' she told their captor firmly. 'Where Paul goes, I go too. Did his mother tell you he needs medical treatments?'

It was a long shot, but one which Amber felt sure had found its mark when the man frowned, swivelling round to study Paul's frail form. Without prompting Paul huddled up against her, and pleaded tearfully, 'My leg hurts . . . it hurts all over. I want my daddy!'

'Okay, okay, you can stay with him. Only keep him quiet, otherwise I'll have to make sure he does keep quiet, understand?'

Amber did, and shuddered to think of drugs being administered forcibly to either of them.

'Aren't you going to blindfold us like they do in the films?' she asked tightly, desperately bargaining for time, praying that someone would return to the Haines' house and start looking for them. But how, and where? No one knew where she was or why they had left.

'That won't be necessary. These roads criss-cross the desert hereabouts and there's so many deserted old shacks that it would take a man a lifetime to search them all. In a few days the boy will be gone. Once the hue and cry dies down his mother plans to fly him out of California and back East where she can sue for American custody as the American parent of a half-American child.'

Amber's heart sank even further. She glanced down at Paul's silky dark head and he lifted his eyes to hers. She squeezed his hand, trying to signify that they couldn't talk, all the time desperately trying to think of some way they could escape—but how?

They drove for another half an hour, by which time she had completely lost her bearings. Her head ached with fear and tension and Paul's face had the waxen pallor of a child about to be car-sick.

'Please stop,' she commanded their captor urgently, 'Paul isn't well.'

To her unutterable relief he obeyed her command, even opening the car door and lifting Paul out into the hot desert air.

'Ten minutes,' he warned them. 'Otherwise you'll both get sunstroke.' He ambled back to the car and bent to select a tape to place into the cassette machine, turning slowly to stare at Amber's rigidly resentful body and add mockingly,

'This is one of the easiest jobs I've had in a long time—kidnapping a pair of cripples. You couldn't run anywhere even if you knew where to run to, could you?'

Tears stung Amber's face as she turned away, but the sudden warm pressure of Paul's hand on hers reminded her that for his sake she had to maintain control.

'Don't cry,' he urged her stoically. 'It will be all right—Dad will come for us.'

Oh, for just a little of Paul's faith!

Their ten minutes was up all too soon and they were hustled back to the car—like a couple of wayward sheep, she thought bitterly as the doors were slammed behind them.

They travelled for another fifteen minutes and then turned off the main road, bouncing down a rough track which ended in front of a delapidated shack, roofed in rusting corrugated iron, the windows grimy and cobwebbed, no signs of life anywhere to be seen.

'Out,' their captor told them curtly, adding to Amber, 'You—you'll find the makings of coffee inside, make some for us while I report back to base.'

Amber saw him fiddle with the two-way radio fixed in the car, and wondered wildly if there was any chance of her getting a message through to someone on it that they had been kidnapped. Probably not, she decided regretfully as she hustled Paul inside the rough shack. The kidnap had been professionally organised by someone who was obviously used to such tasks, and this was confirmed ten minutes later when the door of the shack was thrust open and the driver walked in, sniffing the coffee odour appreciatively, saying, 'That's right. No sense in making things any more difficult than they need to be. Kid's nurse, are you?' he asked, jerking his head towards Paul. 'A cinch, most of these custody cases. Snatch the kid, keep it holed up for long enough for the fuss to die down and then the client ships it off to a state where they can safely sue for their own custody trial.'

'It's horrible!' Amber protested bitterly. 'Don't you care about the misery you're causing, the unfairness . . .'

'It's a business, honey, and I need the pay.' He leaned back in one of the rickety chairs, placing his jean-clad legs on the table and extracting a tin from his pocket. Amber watched him roll a cigarette in silence. There was a tough quality about him that warned her that he was a cynical professional to whom pleading for compassion was a sheer waste of time. Out of the corner of her eye she saw Paul watching him, and reminded herself that her first duty must be to allay the little boy's fears.

'Don't worry,' she whispered to him, crouching down beside him and placing a consoling arm round his thin, hunched shoulders.

'I'm not,' he told her stoutly, 'I know Dad will come. And you needn't be afraid either, I'll look after you.'

'That's the way, son,' their captor jeered. 'Always remember to protect your womenfolk. Don't you want to go and live with your ma? By the sounds of it, she's one hell of a rich lady.'

'I don't like her,' Paul said stubbornly. 'And she doesn't want me really.'

'Sure she wants you. She wants you ten thousand dollars' worth.'

'Is that supposed to make him feel better?' Amber demanded fiercely when Paul's bottom lip trembled, reminding her of just how young he was. 'His mother deserted him. The only reason she wants him is because she wants to hurt his father. Look,' she added desperately, 'his father would pay you the ten thousand dollars to return him, I know he would . . .'

'Sorry, lady.' He was shaking his head. 'One of the first rules of this game is stick with your principal—that way you get more business. Like any other business you've got to build on your reputation—recommendations, see, and if word gets out that you double-deal it's a real no-no!'

He was implacable and uncaring. She and Paul were just a commodity; she was probably lucky he simply hadn't thrown her out of the car when he stopped it earlier, she reflected.

'Why don't you make us a meal?' he suggested, breaking in upon Amber's thoughts. 'It will help keep your mind off things. I won't hurt either of you—that's not the name of the game.'

'How long are you going to keep us here?' Amber asked dryly, moving slowly from the rough wooden table to the old-fashioned oven. Already the shack was becoming unbearably hot, and Paul looked dreadfully pale. Heat didn't agree with young children, and she was terrified that the shock of their kidnapping might undo all the good work they had achieved on his leg.

'That depends. Three or four days possibly for the boy, and I'm not sure about you. The instructions were to dump you somewhere out of the way. It may be that you'll have to stay on here with me after the kid goes to give his ma time to get him clear. Can't have you running back to Daddy telling tales, can we?'

The afternoon wore on interminably. The shack was hot and stuffy. Amber couldn't touch the meal she had made from the canned food in the cupboards. The routine was obviously a familiar one to their captor, and Amber found herself wondering how many times he had acted as watchdog like this while somewhere one parent went frantic with fear and worry, and the other gloated.

She had known all along somewhere deep within her that Teri would attempt something like this, but knowing that she had been right gave her no satisfaction. She remembered how Joel had disappeared with his ex-wife at the party. She had feared then that Teri might be attempting a reconciliation. Muddled, terrified thoughts chased one another through her tired brain.

Darkness came swiftly, stalking the desolate landscape. Paul looked exhausted, and while Amber coaxed him into having a sketchy wash with the water she had heated in the kettle one half of her mind marvelled that she should find it so essential to maintain some travesty of their normal routine, while the other acknowledged that only by clinging to this precarious normality could she retain her own sanity.

Their captor disappeared outside announcing that he was radioing his principal, and Paul stared hopefully towards the car, his breathed, 'Let's try to escape while he's gone,' the small boy's first admission that Joel might not after all find them.

'We can't, Paul,' she told him gently. 'It would be too dangerous. We might get lost and wander round and round in circles never getting any further.'

The sound of the car door closing warned Amber that their guard was on his way back.

'Why didn't you tell me you were married to the kid's father?' he demanded curtly of Amber, stubbing out a cigarette and frowning.

'Why didn't you know, if your organisation is so professional?' Amber retorted, trying to shrug carelessly as she added, 'What does it matter anyway?'

'One hell of a lot, as it happens. His mother might be prepared to guarantee the safety of her kid, but she sure as hell don't feel the same way about you. Orders are that you're to be dumped,' he told Amber cruelly, eyeing her assessingly as he drawled, 'Of course, I might just be persuaded to be . . . flexible.'

'I thought you said you weren't going to hurt us—either of us,' Amber reminded him bitterly.

He shrugged, his eyes narrowed on her flushed face, calloused fingers gripping the side of her throat as he murmurd softly, 'Who's talking about hurting anyone, honey? All I'm talking about here is a little straight bargaining. It's a long time since I've had a beautiful woman in my bed—at least one who isn't a paid whore, and something tells me you're far from being that.'

The way his eyes ran over her made Amber hot and cold with loathing and distaste, her flesh crawling at the thought of him touching her; or anyone touching her apart from Joel. Joel! Her heart and mind cried out for him. What was he doing right now? Worrying about Paul, of course.

'What was that?'

Amber jumped as she was pushed back against the wall, while their guard reached inside his leather jacket and emerged with a gun.

'Stay here,' he warned Amber and Paul, 'and don't make a sound. On second thoughts——' He reached for Paul suddenly, clamping an arm round the struggling boy and half carrying him in front of him, pushed open the door.

In the silence of the desert night, the growing roar of a car engine seemed unnaturally loud, and Amber held her breath as it gradually grew closer, her fingers clenched in unconscious supplication, which turned to fear as she realised that the car was heading for the shack, and that whoever was in it might unwittingly endanger Paul.

At last, unable to bear the suspense, she hurried outside. Moonlight illuminated the small plateau. An unfamiliar car screeched to a halt, kicking up a miniature sand whirlwind. A woman emerged from the car and started to run towards Paul. Amber caught her breath. Teri!

And then, before she could reach the little boy, another figure emerged from the car; tall and imposingly male, his features clearly delineated by the sharp moonlight.

Amber felt sickness well up inside her. Joel! And with Teri. Had she agreed to a reconciliation—was that why Joel was with her? She couldn't bear to look as the two figures converged on the man holding Paul, and turned away, shaken by nausea. A male hand on her shoulder filled her with wild hope, until she turned and recognised Chet's pleasant features.

'You okay?' he asked with concern.

'Fine,' she assured him. 'I'd just like to get away from here.'

'Sure. My car's behind Joel's, I'll take you back to Fairlea if you like.'

'Fairlea?' Amber was too bewildered by the sudden change of events to fully comprehend what was happening. All she did know was that she mustn't glance across to where Joel was standing with Teri, and their son!

'Yeah, Joel's made arrangements to have you and Paul both checked over. God, Teri must have been mad to think she could get away with this. I thought Joel was going to kill her!'

It was almost midnight by the time the doctors had finished examining her and still there was no sign of Joel or Paul.

'You've had a nasty shock,' the doctor sympathised. 'I want to keep you in overnight just to make sure there's no lasting damage. We'll give you a sleeping pill it will help you relax . . .'

Amber started to protest, but she was whisked firmly away by a competent nurse, who handed her the pill and stood over her while she took it, helping her to undress and ensuring that she was firmly tucked up in bed before leaving her.

'Joel . . .' Amber tried to murmur, tears stinging her eyes with sudden remembered pain. 'I . . .'

'You just go to sleep, Mrs Sinclair,' she was told. 'You can see your husband in the morning.'

'Amber . . .'

The voice reached her through a thick cotton-woolly cloud. She tried to lift her head, but it felt too heavy, a strange inertia paralysing her body.

'Amber!'

She opened her eyes and turned her head warily. For some reason her subconscious associated the pleasant male voice with pain. Shock and remembrance jolted through her as she met cool grey eyes.

'So you are with us. Dr James told me they gave you a sleeping pill last night.'

'Joel, where's Paul?' she asked huskily, her eyes searching the room.

'He's fine. They kept him in overnight too, but unlike you he seems to have survived his ordeal without any ill effects. Nurse Adams told me you talked halfway through the night, although she couldn't make much sense of what you were saying.'

Which was probably just as well, Amber thought humbly, as dim recollections of tortured dreams of losing Joel flooded her mind.

'I've made arrangements for us to return home tomorrow,' Joel told her abruptly, his back to her so that she could read nothing in his expression. 'We've got things to talk about, Amber, things I've evaded for too long.'

Amber's heart plummeted. What did he mean? Was he taking Teri back, and if so what about her new husband? He loved Paul, she knew that, and perhaps Teri had used the small child to force his hand. Her head ached with trying to bring order to her chaotic thoughts.

Dr James came in later in the morning and sat on the edge of her bed, watching her for several seconds before he spoke. 'Okay now?' he asked her, adding almost casually, 'By the way, I think we can do something for that leg of yours, if you still want to go ahead?'

Amber shook her head. What did a little thing like her leg matter now? She almost laughed aloud at the irony of her own thoughts; almost, but not quite!

Edie and Lee came to see her later in the day, and Amber guessed that they had been warned by Joel not to let her question them. Edie avoided her eyes, and seemed pale and strained, and Amber felt sure she had been right, and the matter Joel had talked about evading was an admission that he still loved his ex-wife; still loved her and still wanted her, which left Amber herself ... where precisely?

She had known from the start that their relationship had no hope of permanence, Amber reminded herself, and while it was true that Joel had physically desired her; it had been no more than any virile man's desire for a woman with whom he lived intimately.

They flew in to Manchester Airport two days later. Amber had slept for most of the flight, waking to find with dismay that she had been leaning against Joel's shoulder. She had removed herself quickly, but not before she had seen the look in his eyes and been even more convinced that he no longer wanted her—in any capacity.

The house felt cold and damp when they walked in; an abrupt change from the heat of California, and yet somehow Amber felt more at home here. Perhaps the thin grey mizzle of rain soaking the hills was more attuned to her own greyness of spirit.

While Joel switched on the central heating she made a cup of tea. Of all of them Paul seemed to have survived the flight best. His ordeal had, as Joel had told her, left him completely unscathed, although she noticed that every time he started to talk about it, Joel frowned him down. How would Paul react to living with his mother again? she wondered.

They were back three days before Joel broached the subject he had first mentioned in the hospital at Fairlea, and during those three days Amber had clung foolishly to the hope that he would never broach it.

He approached her after dinner and asked her if she could spare him half an hour in the study.

Her heart as heavy as lead, Amber followed him. He motioned her into a chair and stood for a moment frowning down at her.

'Amber, this isn't easy for me to do,' he said at last. 'God knows I've been unfair to you all through this damned mess, but after what happened with Paul ...' He raked disturbed fingers through his hair. 'What I'm trying to say is that I'm setting you free, Amber.' He wouldn't look at her, and Amber couldn't look at him for fear of what her eyes might reveal. She heard the sound of a drawer being opened and then closed, and then Joel said abruptly, 'Here. I know I said twenty-five thousand originally, but ...'

Amber's head lifted, her face pale as she stared at the cheque he had pushed towards her.

'Fifty thousand!'

'Call it conscience money. It will help pay some of those medical bills.'

'Yes,' Amber agreed bitterly, telling herself that

the searing pain she was experiencing couldn't possibly last for ever, and that all she had to do was simply to grit her teeth until it subsided. 'Who knows,' she added gallantly, 'perhaps once I'm whole again Rob might change his mind.' She stood up, pinning a smile to her face, the cheque in her hand, her head held high as she walked out.

Upstairs in her room she tore it into tiny pieces and dropped them into the wastepaper bin. Then she locked herself in the bathroom where her tears could mingle with the stinging spray of the shower without anyone but herself being aware that she was shedding them. Joel had bought her off! The pain of it was more than she could bear. If he hadn't offered her that money she could have stood it—which was silly really when she thought of how she had originally accepted his proposition because he had offered her money—at least on the surface. But she had come to love him and had thought mistakenly that he had some respect for her. How wrong she had been. Now that Teri was back in his life, he couldn't wait to get rid of her!

She stepped out of the shower and wrapped herself in a towel, too weary to bother drying herself properly, merely walking drearily into the bedroom, and coming to a shocked standstill in front of the bed.

Joel was sitting on it, arms folded against his chest. Ever since their return from America they had been sleeping apart, and it was almost more than she could bear that he should come here now, when she was at her most vulnerable.

'Joel!' Her hand crept to her throat in a defensive gesture. 'What . . . what are you doing here?'

'You left before we'd finished our conversation.'

'What do you want?' she demanded bitterly. 'A signed declaration of when I'm going to leave? I'll go now if you like! What's the matter—doesn't Teri trust me with you?'

She paused. Joel wasn't even looking at her. His eyes were on the torn up pieces of cheque in the waste-paper bin.

'Why did you do that?' he asked softly.

Just for a moment she was tempted to tell him because it hadn't been enough, but the impulse died, to be replaced with a weariness that made her admit, 'Perhaps because my pride wouldn't allow me to accept it.'

'Not even when it could have bought you your operation? Dr James told me all about it. That was why you accepted my proposition in the first place, wasn't it?'

'Yes.' She could admit it now.

'So why destroy it now? Or has Rob come to his senses and wants you back regardless of your leg?'

'Rob?'

'Yes,' Joel drawled, his voice suddenly dangerously soft. 'You remember—the man you loved. The man you were thinking about when I made love to you.'

'Just as you were thinking about Teri!' Amber flung at him. 'Well, you've got her back now, haven't you? And you want me out of your life. Well, don't worry—I'm going. I . . .'

'I want Teri back?' He stared at her in furious incredulity. 'Have you gone mad? I damn near killed her when I discovered the little stunt she'd tried to pull. When I got back and discovered you and Paul were missing I nearly lost my mind. I saw Chet's name on the phone pad and a number, and I thought you'd gone off with him—he made it pretty plain that he wouldn't have objected—what sane man would?' he breathed smokily. 'God, when I think of the mental agony I endured when Chet came over and told me you said you were taking Paul to the hospital, after we discovered that you weren't there. And then we checked the phone number and discovered it was allocated to a detective agency; that was when I began to put two and two together.'

'You mean you and Teri . . .'

'Teri and I are finished,' he told her brutally, 'and if you'd listened to one half of what I've been telling you you'd know there's only one woman for me, and she's standing right here in front of me,' he added huskily, bending his head to lick the droplets of moisture from her skin, his eyes darkening suddenly with desire as his mouth left her bare shoulder and fastened hungrily on hers. Fierce pleasure burned inside her, her arms reached up for him, her fingers tangling in the thick dark hair as she pressed herself into the warmth of his body, pliant under the fierce pressure of his kiss, answering it with a passion of her own, until they were both trembling. With a wry grimace Joel held her away from him.

'Don't tell me you're still in any doubt as to how I feel about you?' he asked her sardonically. 'And if it feeds your ego you might as well know that concerned as I was for Paul; it was the thought of you being hurt that drove me to threaten to expose what Teri had attempted to do to Lee if she didn't tell me where you were. She

broke then, after wasting precious minutes denying that she knew anything about your dis-
appearance. But Lee had no idea what she
planned to do.'

'I thought you still loved her, especially when
you disappeared with her at the party.'

'When she dragged me off, don't you mean?
And the only reason I went with her was to protect
you from her malicious tongue. And how do you
reward me? By dancing with another man in a way
that made me long to tear him limb from limb.
I've always prided myself on being a thinking
human being, but you destroyed all that when you
reduced me to a purely sensual male animal,
fiercely possessive of the woman he loved. If I
hadn't stopped making love to you when I did
after that party, I couldn't have lived with
myself . . .'

'I thought you stopped because you didn't love
me,' Amber told him, smiling tremulously at his
huskily growled imprecation.

'You were the one who didn't love me,' he told
her.

'I did, right from the start, but I was so obsessed
about my leg that I couldn't see it.'

'Dr James told me that you'd decided against
having the operation. That's why I offered to pay
for it for you. I wanted to give you something,
even if you wouldn't allow me to give you my
love.'

'When I realised that I loved you, my leg didn't
seem important,' Amber told him simply, 'and I
couldn't bear to think that you'd bought me off,
casually disposed of me so that you could take up
your old life with Teri.'

'What life? There's only one woman I want in my life, and she's right here in my arms. I wanted you right from the start; the first time I saw you looking so vulnerable but acting so tough. I told myself you were just another mercenary little bitch, but when I saw you with Paul I knew that wasn't true. God knows I fought against loving you. I told myself that you were just a means of ensuring that I got Paul, but deep down inside I knew it wasn't true. You'll never know how many times I had to force myself to keep on working downstairs when all I longed to do was to come up here and do this . . .'

He slid the towel from her shoulders, laughing at the faint colour staining her cheeks at his frank appreciation of her naked form. And then he bent his head, tenderly touching his lips to hers, while Amber clung unashamedly to him, revelling in the racing thud of his heart against hers, her fingers finding the open neck of his shirt.

'Amber!' Her fingers were trapped, molten desire flaming in the look he gave her.

'Our marriage begins tonight,' he told her huskily, lifting her and carrying her effortlessly towards the bed. 'And I promise you I'll teach you the true meaning of the words "with my body I thee worship"—starting right here!'

He bent swiftly to cup the delicate arch of her foot, kissing the soft skin. With a murmured protest, half delight, half despair, Amber tugged on his arm, and as though he understood her overriding need to be held next to his body and be succoured by it, his arms tightened around her.

'Tell me you love me,' he demanded urgently against her lips.

'I love you,' she said simply. 'And I want you so much it *hurts*!'

'Tell me where,' he murmured, 'and I'll kiss it better. I've got some aching scars of my own.'

He was everything she had ever dreamed of finding in a man, and where she had once cursed her accident because it had cost her Rob, now she blessed it, because it had brought her Joel and a far greater love than the pale emotion she would have known with Rob had she ever become his wife.

'I want you, Amber,' Joel whispered urgently against her skin. 'Love me.'

His touch was like a lighted tinder applied to dry brushwood, the resultant inferno threatening to destroy her every last barrier, but with Joel she was safe, and knowing that she gave herself up willing to the desire consuming them both, winding her arms round his neck and abandoning herself completely to him.

ENGLAND'S BEAUTIFUL LAKE DISTRICT

Serene lakes with such names as Derwent Water, Buttermere, Thirlmere and Bassenthwaite nestle at the foot of verdant slopes. Towering high above are craggy peaks of mauve gray rock. Unlike the gently undulating countryside of most of England, the Lake District is a wild and rugged place, filled with the magnificent bounty of nature. Situated in northwestern England, in the county of Cumbria, the Lake District is so small an area that a motorist can traverse it in a day; yet it contains England's largest national park, its biggest lakes, highest mountains (which are also the world's oldest) and more than enough territory to explore in a lifetime.

Besides the natural beauty, there are remnants of many periods of history here: the prehistoric stone circles at Castlerigg and Swinside; the stone mound or "cairn" at Dunmail Raise, said to be the burial mound of the last king of Cumbria; the old Roman forts near Ravenglass, Hardknott and Borrans; the roads that carried the Roman legions north to defend Britain from Scottish barbarians, still traveled between the quaint towns of Kendal, Penrith and Carlisle; the hillside ruins of ancient abbeys; and in villages, the restored medieval castles, which are now private homes.

It is little wonder that the area, with its natural beauty and fascinating history, has attracted many artists and writers. Beatrix Potter, the creator of Peter Rabbit, resided near Hawkshead. And the great nineteenth-century poet William Wordsworth lived most of his life among its hills. Surely when he wrote that "nature never did betray the heart that loved her," he was inspired by nothing other than England's beautiful Lake District!

Take these
4 best-selling novels
FREE